"Who's the tall Navajo man in the brown leather jacket with a pistol on his hip?"

"That's Daniel Hawk," Holly's contact said, following her gaze. "Hawk conducts our training exercises, not only here, but also at every critical tribal facility. Naturally he's got the highest clearance level."

Holly nodded, finally being able to put a face to the name. She'd heard Daniel Hawk described as a one-time bad boy who could attract women faster than free chocolate. Daniel had *presence.* That confidence and take-charge attitude, coupled with those wide shoulders and long legs, sure made him easy on the eyes.

She watched Daniel Hawk as he moved, his back straight, his steps measured and filled with purpose. He came to a stop and glanced around the room, his gaze missing nothing. Then, for a brief moment, his eyes met hers. His steady, penetrating look was a blend of curiosity and casual sensuality that made her body tingle all over.

Yet it wasn't admir... ...ed in the dark e... ...ubtle challenge.

AIMÉE THURLO

WINTER HAWK'S LEGEND

TORONTO NEW YORK LONDON
AMSTERDAM PARIS SYDNEY HAMBURG
STOCKHOLM ATHENS TOKYO MILAN MADRID
PRAGUE WARSAW BUDAPEST AUCKLAND

To Sydney Abernathy, the best assistant—ever. May your future be
bright, and may you always walk with beauty before you.

Recycling programs
for this product may
not exist in your area.

ISBN-13: 978-0-373-69583-6

WINTER HAWK'S LEGEND

Copyright © 2011 by Aimée and David Thurlo

ABOUT THE AUTHOR

Aimée Thurlo is a nationally known bestselling author. She's the winner of a Career Achievement Award from *RT Book Reviews*, a New Mexico Book Award in contemporary fiction and a Willa Cather Award in the same category. Her novels have been published in twenty countries worldwide.

She also cowrites the bestselling Ella Clah mainstream mystery series praised in the *New York Times* Book Review.

Aimée was born in Havana, Cuba, and lives with her husband of thirty-nine years in Corrales, New Mexico. Her husband, David, was raised on the Navajo Indian Reservation.

Books by Aimée Thurlo

HARLEQUIN INTRIGUE

Don't miss any of our special offers. Write to us at the following address for information on our newest releases.

Harlequin Reader Service
U.S.: 3010 Walden Ave., P.O. Box 1325, Buffalo, NY 14269
Canadian: P.O. Box 609, Fort Erie, Ont. L2A 5X3

CAST OF CHARACTERS

Daniel Hawk—His job was to keep Holly Gates alive, but he'd never factored falling in love into the equation. Christmas was fast approaching and a killer was on their trail. With everything on the line, win or lose, Daniel knew his life would never be the same again.

Holly Gates—She had an enemy, a man determined to see her dead. The only person standing between her and the grave was temptation itself—a sexy but dangerous security expert with a clear future—but a clouded past.

Martin Roanhorse—He was their boss, at least on paper, and knew everything about them. He was definitely part of the problem, but he was also hiding secrets of his own that could cost them all.

Arthur Larrabee—An ex-cop running for city council, Art was also a security consultant who operated on the principle that the best defense against intruders was overwhelming violence. That made him a potential liability to his clients, including the tribe.

Johnny Wauneka—The young hacker had his own agenda, and Holly, the tribal publicist, was near the top of his enemies list. Was he out to kill the beautiful Anglo woman, or just her message?

Gene Redhouse—He was Daniel's foster brother. Even if it meant leaving his beloved ranch in a neighbor's hands, he had Daniel's back.

Clyde Keesewood—The Navajo activist was an angry man with a mission. The last time they'd met he'd threatened Holly in front of a hundred witnesses. Did he do that just for show, or did he walk his talk?

Ross Williams—The sleazy salesman had decided that Holly was the woman for him. He never passed up an opportunity to corner her, publicly or privately, and Ross didn't handle rejection well.

Joe Yazzie—Martin's tribal assistant appeared to be the perfect patsy after his security lapses put everyone in danger. He was either careless, or taking part in a larger plan only he could know.

all six was strong, forged by the man who'd refused to believe that any Navajo boy could be truly bad.

Hosteen Silver had turned their lives around, two at a time, teaching them what was important in life and how to assume responsibility. Preston was a cop in Hartley, a small city just off the reservation. Paul, a U.S. Deputy Marshal, had recently distinguished himself by saving the life of a federal judge. Kyle was serving with NCIS overseas, and Rick.... No one except Daniel knew what he really did for the FBI, and he'd only found out by accident when Rick had needed help.

Hosteen Silver had been proud of them all, though he'd shown that by example, not words. Yet what bound them as a family went beyond blood ties. It was love for the man who'd given them a chance—a handhold on life.

"Are you thinking that there's a reason he wanted us to work together here, something that goes beyond returning the fetish?"

"Yeah. He had a way of seeing trouble coming," Daniel said, struggling up to the next narrow outcropping. "I think he wanted us to renew a bond he thought might have weakened since we've gone our own ways."

"He was always concerned that we'd lose touch, and our family connection. He knew that over time, the ties that bind can loosen—come undone."

"I tried to tell him that would never happen, even if one of us moved to the moon," Daniel said. "We share too much history."

"Back at the foster home, you and I were the only Navajo kids and that made us targets. I was sick a lot back then, but you always had my back."

"I enjoyed taking those guys on. Then *Hosteen* Silver came into our lives. We went from the frying pan into the fire. We were out of that environment, but remember how he worked our butts off?" Daniel said, chuckling.

"I think that's what made me healthy again. I finally had clean air, and plenty of exercise, physical and mental."

"Once you could fight your own battles, your confidence shot way up."

"And we started competing big-time," Gene said, laughing. "Last time I saw *Hosteen* Silver, he asked if we still enjoyed pushing each other's buttons. I told him we'd grown way past that, but I don't think he believed me."

"Maybe that's part of the reason he sent us here to deliver his final gift to Winter Hawk. The only way we'd make it all the way up was if we worked together," Daniel said.

Daniel reached for Gene, steadying him as another foothold crumbled, the chunks of sandstone tumbling into the air, then cascading to the rocks far below. "We're almost there. If I'm right, the shelf we want is back to the left and up. You better take the lead now."

After several minutes inching forward, Gene stopped and looked up. The hawk gazed down at him. "Don't make any sudden moves or loud noises," he whispered to Daniel.

They were less than ten feet away from the nest now. "Do you remember the legend?" Gene asked, waiting where he was and giving the bird a chance to settle before drawing closer.

"Word for word. It was one of the first stories *Hosteen* Silver ever told us," Daniel said, his soft voice resonating with echoes from the past. "Hawk and his mate always honored their true natures. When they came home every night, they'd take human form and be clothed in garments of bright light. *Hosteen* Silver would then tell us that, like Hawk, we had the power to change at a moment's notice and become the men we wanted to be. The choice was ours to make."

The story seemed to energize Gene. He reached for a new handhold on a sturdy-looking scrub oak, but the plant suddenly came out by the roots. Gene slipped, and for a brief instant, swayed back and forth as he gripped the rock with his left hand only.

"Hang on!" Daniel reached for Gene, steadied his swing, then pulled him upward to a firm foothold.

"Okay, I've got it now," Gene said, his breathing labored.

Daniel waited, giving Gene a chance to catch his breath. "We were so bad back then. Everyone said we were no good— just plain trouble—so we had to live up to the reputation. Then came *Hosteen* Silver." He chuckled, the sound deep and rumbling.

"Careful, bro. Don't let Winter Hawk misinterpret your tone."

The bird lifted her wings, as if to fly, then, as Gene began a *Hozonji,* a soft, deep Song of Blessing, settled down again and started preening.

"Go past me. I'm too close, and I don't like the way that bird's eyeing me," Daniel said.

"She's just trying to figure out what we're up to, that's all," Gene said softly, reaching into his jacket pocket and moving along the shelf as Daniel hugged the rock wall.

Daniel watched his brother as he held out the medicine bag with the fetish, and moving ever so slowly, placed it inside the nest.

The hawk hopped back a step, but didn't fly away.

Daniel smiled. "Had it been me, I'd have pulled back a bloodied stump."

"It's your approach. First you have to show respect."

"I respect what Hawk is—a raptor, a bird of prey," Daniel said.

"No, not just a bird. Hawk is connected spiritually to our family. By honoring that, we walk in beauty."

Daniel watched the bird peck and probe the bag for a few seconds, then settle back down, reassured.

"Winter Hawk accepts the tribute," Gene said.

"We're done, then," Daniel said, turning to search for the foothold below his current position.

"No, it's not over," Gene said, resting his face against the cold sandstone, then looking down at Daniel. "Trouble *is* coming. *Hosteen* Silver was never wrong about things like that."

Daniel knew Gene was right. He could feel it in his bones. "We'll face it when it comes, bro, and when the dust settles, we'll still be standing. Count on it."

Chapter One

Holly Gates was running ahead of schedule this morning so, on impulse, she decided to turn off the highway and take the old dirt road that ran through the backcountry. This route circled an area of rolling hills filled with fragrant piñon trees, then connected with the natural gas plant's access road—her destination.

The brilliant blue sky and the unseasonably warm December weather here in northwestern New Mexico made it a perfect morning. Mountains dotted with gray-green forests rose to the north and west. The long, table mesa to the east was lined with cliffs colored in deep reds, orange and even layers of violet, like a sandstone sunrise.

Smiling, Holly looked around the brush and low trees for cottontails, quail and whatever else might be out and about. A solitary red-tailed hawk circled above, watchful for an inattentive rodent or bird.

There were few perfect moments in life, but out here in nature she felt completely at ease. Some people chased happiness as if it were a destination. Yet over the years, she'd learned that happiness could also be found in a well-planned journey. Everyday decisions could become building blocks for an even better tomorrow for those with the foresight to work with an eye on the future.

The courage to nurture her hopes and dreams, along with a lot of hard work, had brought her to where she was today. Just as she knew precisely where she was heading this morning, she also knew where her goals would eventually take her.

At twenty-seven, she owned her own business here in New Mexico. TechTalk Incorporated offered consulting and public relations services to its clients. Currently, she was working almost exclusively on a project with the largest tribe in the U.S., the Navajo Nation. What made her services invaluable was her ability to explain highly technical scientific data in everyday English.

Movement off to the left of the graveled road caught her eye. At a glance she could see several grayish-tan coyotes moving at a fast trot, perpendicular to her route. It was a family group probably—three of the five were clearly smaller than the two mature adults at the front and rear of the pack.

Holly slowed to a crawl for a closer look. She rarely got a chance to study coyotes up close. Navajos, she knew, avoided these creatures, considering them bad luck. Coyote, in the Navajo creation stories, was known as The Trickster and, at best, was an undependable ally.

Holly stopped just before the top of a small rise. If she ventured too close, the human-wise coyotes would alter course and disappear into the brush. As she turned off the engine and set the brake, a flash of color and movement to her left caught her eye.

In a small patch of open ground, a bearded man wearing a baseball cap was unloading a pick from the back of a black, newer-model hardtop Jeep. On the ground beside him was a large, green, military-style canvas duffel bag. Not far beyond, she could see a big hole with a mound of freshly dug earth beside it.

Perhaps responding to the sudden lack of engine noise and crunch of tires on gravel, he turned around and gave her the once-over. Holly waved, greeting him with a smile.

Frowning, the man set the pick down on the ground, propped the handle against the tailgate, then walked away.

Either he wasn't the friendly type, or he was just plain tired from digging and in no mood to socialize. Of course if he'd needed a pick to break the crust of the hard-packed ground, he probably had his hands full. Judging from the college parking sticker with its big red F on its rear window and his neatly groomed beard, she figured that he was either an archeology or geology professor from the local college.

Though he hadn't been friendly, Holly scarcely gave it a thought. She always waved at people and greeted them like old friends. She'd learned a long time ago that a smile and a wave could open doors, or at the very least, disarm a potential enemy.

As a new business owner, her friendliness and upbeat nature were an even greater asset to her now. Even a casual wave that called attention to her became added publicity, a method of networking. Her company's name, TechTalk Incorporated, along with the telephone number and website address, were painted on the driver's-side door of her pickup. Since she had no extra funds to pay for advertising, this was an inexpensive way of getting attention and potential clients.

When Holly looked back down the road, searching for the coyotes, she found that they'd already disappeared—a survival skill that served them well. Switching on the ignition, she glanced back at the man. The professor or student was by his Jeep again, struggling to load the heavy green duffel bag into the back. For a second she wondered if she should offer to help, but as she reached for the ignition key to turn off the engine again, the man completed the task.

He was probably a geologist with a bag of rock samples. An archeologist would have wrapped up and handled his unearthed find more carefully.

Holly glanced at her watch. It was time for her to get going.

Ten minutes later, she arrived at the gate of the Navajo tribe's New Horizon Energy's secure facility. The natural gas processing plant piped in raw natural gas, cleaned it of contaminants, then sent it downline to be used as fuel by consumers. Three strands of barbed wire stood at the top of the mesh, which surrounded the several-acre facility. Security at energy facilities was always high, but she was getting used to it.

Holly handed her photo ID to the armed, uniformed, middle-aged Navajo man at the guardhouse and gave him a smile. Bruce was barrel-chested and about fifty pounds overweight, but she doubted anyone could knock him down without a lot of help.

"Good morning, young lady," he said with a broad smile. "You all ready for Christmas?"

"If that's a hint, I'll be making those chocolate cake cookies you love in a day or two. You'll be my first stop."

"My wife would love that recipe—if you ever change your mind."

"Sorry," Holly said with a smile. "The pastry chef who came up with it made me swear to never tell a soul. She owns a catering business in Texas now."

"I'm sure those cookies paved the way for her, too."

Holly waited until Bruce scanned her ID's bar code into his handheld device, and wrote her arrival time on his clipboard. Once he gave her a nod, she drove through and nosed her pickup into her designated employee parking space.

Holly walked to the next, unmanned checkpoint, used her access card and went inside the administration building. She could see people gathering in the conference room already, but it was mostly around the coffee and doughnut table, so she would have time to review her notes. She took an aisle seat in the front row and opened her briefcase.

Today she was scheduled to present an overview of the proposed new natural gas recovery process to area guests, industry people, and state and local government representatives. Afterward, she'd give the community leaders who had sufficient clearance a tour of the facility.

Holly saw Martin Roanhorse, the tribal department head,

at the front of the room speaking with the facility manager. She was glad that Martin approved of her work, but she hated the way he'd often give her assignments at the last minute. He'd never understood how much preparation her presentations actually took, especially when the audience included both PhD-level engineers and local media who preferred information in sound bites.

Spotting her, Martin hurried over, arriving just as she opened her folder. As usual, he was well dressed. Today, his bolo tie complemented his brown wool Western suit and his snakeskin boots were shined to perfection.

"Here's an update on our guest list, Holly," he said. "We've made some last-minute additions. We've expanded this event to include several people from the public sector. I've listed the occupation of each participant, as well as their stated reason for attending," Martin said, ignoring her scowl. "The tour of the facility, of course, will remain restricted to those who've already been cleared."

"I've asked you before *not* to spring these things on me at the last minute, Martin. Half of what I've already prepared will probably go right over their heads. I'm supposed to communicate, not confuse."

"I know, and I'm sorry about that, but this request came from the tribal president. He's been getting flak from some activists and wanted you to make sure everyone understood that there's no danger to the aquifer."

She took a deep breath and let it out again. "The new guests… Is that why I'm seeing extra security this morning?" Holly cocked her head toward the back of the room where two plant security guards were stationed just inside the exit.

"Yeah," he said. "Don't worry. Everyone was checked with the wands when they came through the security gates."

"Who's the tall Navajo man in the brown leather jacket with a pistol on his hip? A tribal cop? He looks ex-military."

"You may have heard his name mentioned during tribal

agency meetings. That's Daniel Hawk," he said, following her gaze. "Like you, he's a private consultant. Hawk owns Level One Security and conducts our training exercises, not only here, but also at every critical tribal facility. Naturally he's got the highest clearance level."

Holly nodded, finally being able to place a face to the name. She'd heard Daniel Hawk described as a one-time bad boy who could attract women faster than free chocolate. Daniel had *presence*. That confidence and take-charge attitude, coupled with those wide shoulders and long legs, sure made him easy on the eyes.

She watched Daniel Hawk as he moved, his back straight, his steps measured and filled with purpose. He came to a stop and glanced around the room, his gaze missing nothing. Then, for a brief moment, his eyes met hers. That steady, penetrating look was a blend of curiosity and casual sensuality that made her body tingle all over.

Holly was used to being checked out by men wherever she was. Though she wasn't drop-dead gorgeous, at five foot three she had generous curves in all the right places and men had a tendency to turn their heads to look when she stepped into a room. Yet it wasn't admiration that was mirrored in the dark eyes that held hers—it was a subtle challenge.

Taking a deep breath, Holly forced herself to look away. He wasn't checking her out in a man-woman sort of way. He was a professional, sizing her up as he would any stranger in his environment.

Hearing herself being introduced, her focus shifted instantly to the job at hand. Holly beamed a confident smile to everyone in the audience as she strode up to the podium. Prepared, she started her presentation without skipping a beat. Martin had already loaded her graphics into the projection system and the remote worked perfectly.

Even though nearly every seat in the room was occupied, she felt completely at ease. Her engaging voice kept everyone's attention, even through the dry, technical segments of her presentation.

Everything went smoothly until she began to explain the specifics of the new extraction process—an improved technique for freeing up deposits of natural gas far below the surface. Out of the corner of her eye Holly saw a Navajo man wearing a denim jacket rise from his seat. He sidestepped past the seated guests and headed toward the center aisle.

Holly wondered if the man was having difficulty keeping up with the technical portion, but she was forced to block him from her mind and focus on her presentation.

As soon as he reached the aisle and turned toward the podium instead of the exit, Holly recognized him instantly. Clyde Keeswood was a community activist who'd opposed the tribe's energy resource operations from day one. He'd shouted out his opposition in every press conference and lecture she'd held the past few months. *Now what?*

Almost as the thought formed, she saw Daniel Hawk on the move.

"This is the same PR bull we hear every day," Keeswood shouted, walking toward her. "Why don't you give us the whole story?" He came to a stop next to her empty chair and glared at her.

"I promise to answer your questions *after* I finish explaining the details of the extraction process," Holly said, refusing to raise her voice. "I'll keep it brief, Mr. Keeswood, then we'll address whatever concerns you have. If you can take a seat...."

He remained standing. "Nothing will be brief, except our way of life after the wells run dry. Sure, the tribe and their big business partners will make gobs of money selling natural gas to— I don't know, big developers, factories? But the water table will be contaminated with chemicals—that's if the wells don't go dry first. You think this is a desert now? Just wait."

"No chemicals except water itself will be used to free up the gas formations. Let me show you how it works," she said.

She stepped to the left and pressed a remote. A projector on the far side of the room produced an image on the screen behind her on the wall.

The man spat out a curse and picked up her chair. As he raised it over his head, Daniel Hawk was suddenly there. In a split second he yanked the chair away from Keeswood.

The force threw the activist off balance. He fell backward and toppled onto the tile floor. Daniel set the chair aside, and straddled the troublemaker, ready to roll him over and cuff him.

Keeswood punched upward but Daniel blocked the jab, grabbed his hand, then twisted it around, forcing the man face-down on the floor. By then, two uniformed security guards arrived. They hauled Keeswood to his feet and quickly led him away.

Barely ten seconds had passed, but the room had grown completely silent. Holly glanced at Daniel, and he nodded, giving her a thumbs-up.

"Harmony has been restored. I think we can continue now," she said, and the room exploded in applause. Holly glanced back, looking for Daniel, but all she saw was his back as he left the room.

Disappointed, she focused on what she had to do. Later, when she could get away, she'd catch up to him and thank him personally for what he'd done.

Chapter Two

Once her presentation came to a close, Holly smiled at her largely enthusiastic audience and thanked the group for their patience. "Now I'd like to answer all your questions. Please ask me whatever you'd like."

The question-and-answer session took another thirty minutes. Afterward, they broke for a well-deserved lunch.

Holly followed the attendees to the small cafeteria at the other end of the building. Going down the buffet line, she opted for a large bowl of fresh mutton stew, warm fry bread and hot coffee in a big white mug with the tribal emblem on the side. With her tray full, she headed to a table by the windows. As she approached the spot, a tingle of awareness spread through her.

Female intuition... She knew even before she could confirm it that Daniel Hawk was looking at her.

As Holly set her tray down, Daniel came up and introduced himself, but according to Navajo customs, didn't offer to shake hands.

"No introduction is necessary, Mr. Hawk," she said, noting how low and masculine the timbre of his voice was and how it seemed to fit him perfectly. "I know who you are and I'm glad you came over." She sat down and invited him to join her. "I owe you a big thank-you."

"No thanks are needed, but I thought you could use some pointers on how to spot trouble before it happens," he said, taking a seat across from her. "We can talk now while you have lunch."

For a moment she wondered if he was somehow blaming her for what had happened. "I'd like to hear what you've got to say," she said, "but my job is to give presentations. If there's a problem, security has to handle it."

"They will. I just thought a few tips might give you an edge. If nothing else, it could give you time to duck."

She smiled, but before she could answer, two more session attendees came up with their trays to join them at the table. They'd only been there a minute or so when Daniel's pager went off and he was forced to leave.

"He's really something, isn't he?" Jennifer Long, a representative from a local utility cooperative, whispered.

Holly watched Daniel until he left the cafeteria. "He's observant, too. I get the feeling very little gets past him."

"Do you suppose he knows he's total eye candy?" Mary Randall, an attorney for the tribe, said with a mischievous smile.

They laughed, and as Holly ate lunch, two more people joined them. It wasn't until later that afternoon, during a pause in the schedule, that Holly saw Daniel again. He met her by the coffee urn as she stepped out of a meeting room during a short break.

"I'm glad we ran into each other," Holly said. "I've been thinking about what you said and I would like to get some of those tips you mentioned. If I remember things right, you were on the move today *before* the trouble with Keeswood began. How did you know what would happen?"

"I watched him from the moment he came into the room. His shoulders were rigid and he looked like a man looking for trouble. I went with my gut and stayed close."

"So it was reading his body language that did it," she said with a nod.

"There was more," he answered. "I noticed that he kept

checking out the location of security with his eyes, but not moving his head to stare directly. This is all part of what I wanted to talk to you about. If you're willing to set aside some time, I'd be happy to teach you a few things."

"I'll be through here at four-thirty. Would you like to meet then?" she said.

He checked his watch, then shook his head. "Sorry, I can't. I've still got two more meetings to attend today. One of them will probably run over, too, since we'll be working out the details of our next security training exercise. How about if we meet for dinner tonight? You name the place?"

She hesitated. She didn't date people associated with her work. That hard-and-fast rule had helped her company run smoothly.

"Please don't think of it as a date. It's business," he said, almost as if he'd read her mind.

She nodded, relieved. "How about we meet at the Simple Pleasures Café in Hartley, off Twentieth Street? Do you know it?"

"I've never been there, but I've passed by. I can meet you at, say, seven?"

As she looked at Daniel, in his weathered brown leather jacket and jeans, she wondered if his tastes ran closer to the Bucking Bronco, just outside of Hartley and a world away from Simple Pleasures.

The Bucking Bronco was a bar and grill well-known for the good ol' boys it attracted. It wasn't a rough place, at least not if you judged solely on the number of police visits per month. The bar, in county jurisdiction, had its own way of handling trouble. She'd heard that disputes there were settled inside a cage until one of the parties went down.

"Seven it is, then," she said, realizing that her thoughts had wandered.

"For what it's worth, I admire how you kept your cool when Keeswood confronted you. It showed courage and character."

He flashed her a heart-stopping half smile, then his gaze shifted. "Martin needs me," he said, giving their boss a nod. "I better get back to work."

"Me, too. Break time's over," she said, looking down at the foam coffee cup she'd never filled.

The rest of the day went by in slow motion. She'd always prided herself on her ability to stay focused, but Daniel Hawk was proving to be a very persistent distraction. She was curious about the man she'd heard women whispering about around the coffee machine. No matter what else, it promised to be an interesting dinner tonight.

HOLLY ARRIVED HOME in Hartley shortly after six. She stepped inside her small, World War II era *casita,* a two-bedroom home in an established middle-class neighborhood, and felt the tranquility of the house welcome her. She'd worked hard to make the fixer-upper place she'd bought two years ago into the home it was today.

She smiled as she looked at the light apricot-colored walls, her favorite color, and the old hardwood floors, worn in the center and slightly concave in places from decades of foot traffic. She'd lovingly refinished the thirties era armoire and the solid oak bookcase to match the honey glow of the tongue and groove floors.

All her furniture had a past and its own history. She'd bought most of the pieces at auctions or estate sales. Each had called to her in a special way, maybe because of an intricate carving in the wood, or the construction itself.

Most important, all her belongings spoke of endurance and stability. Growing up, change had been the only constant in her life. Her father, a gambler usually on the run from creditors, the law, or on the lookout for fresh pigeons, had kept them on the move.

Her own home was a reminder that those days were finally behind her. It was a symbol of permanence and security, the very things that had always eluded her and what she valued most. To the observant, her home's whispers revealed much about her, things she wanted to keep private. Maybe that was why she usually only invited close friends over.

Holly stopped by the big cardboard egg crate that held all her Christmas ornaments. She'd set it against the wall, ready to open up as soon as she brought her Christmas tree home. It would be a six-foot blue spruce this year, with lots of branches. She already had an image of what it would look like in her mind.

Reaching down, she picked up the hand-carved angel she'd placed on top of all the other ornaments. It was a lovely piece signed by a turn-of-the-century Spanish carver in Santa Fe. The other ornaments were also antiques, salvaged here and there from unlikely places. Even the metal stand, though simple in design, dated back to the nineteen-fifties.

As her cherrywood grandfather clock chimed the half hour, Holly hurried into the bedroom. She needed to shower and change before meeting Daniel.

Twenty-five minutes later, she emerged from the bedroom wearing a simple emerald-green turtleneck sweater and dark, comfortable wool pants. Grabbing her coat from the rack as she left, she set out.

It was a perfect evening, so she'd decided to walk to Simple Pleasures. The night temperature was unseasonably warm, and tonight there was going to be a meteor shower. The chance of seeing a shooting star was too good to pass up.

Though it was still early in the evening and she knew that most celestial activity would be after midnight, she kept her eyes on the heavens as she walked. The cloudless sky would make it easy to see nature's light show. The streets here were dark enough for that, with streetlamps only at the intersections between blocks. No one minded, since the neighborhood was as safe as could be.

Although the south side of the boulevard beginning at

the end of the block was zoned commercial, ordinances re-stricted light pollution and business signs. The coffee shop on the corner and the converted homes beyond served mostly as law and real estate professional offices and didn't shout their presence.

There was no traffic at the moment, so Holly decided to leave the sidewalk and cross diagonally. There was a big pine tree in the median and she loved its Christmassy scent. As she stepped out into the street, Holly heard footsteps approaching from behind.

She turned, ready to greet a person she assumed would be one of her neighbors—but she was wrong. A man wearing some kind of dark bandanna over his face lunged toward her. His eyes gleamed in the moonlight as he grabbed her hard by the shoulders, pulling her close.

"Let go!" she yelled, pushing him in the chest as hard as she could.

Holly tried to scream, but a heavy glove quickly covered her mouth, cutting off her breath. The man spun her around, wrapped his free arm across her middle like a vise, then dragged her over the curb and onto the grass between the trees. When she kicked him in the leg, he lifted her off the ground, leaving her flailing in midair.

Grunting, he pushed her face down into the grass, his knees on her back. He smelled of sweat and strong aftershave, and his weight was crushing the air right out of her lungs. For a moment his hand slipped off her mouth and she screamed as loud as she could.

Holly felt him slip the loop of heavy cord over her head and knew he intended to strangle her. She was in a fight for her life. Terrified, she scrunched her chin against her chest and slipped her hand up under the cord, trying to keep it away from her throat. Her fingers pressed into her throat painfully, but if she wanted to live, she had to keep them in the way. It was her only hope.

Chapter Three

Daniel turned into the alley and parked his SUV in the rear lot of Simple Pleasures. The coffee shop—a former home—was off the street and had a big front porch with dining tables underneath for warmer weather and sunny days.

He pressed the key button remote to lock the car and wondered if he was early or late. When he was off the clock he preferred to go on Indian time, but he had a feeling that Holly was the kind of woman who appreciated promptness. It was certainly a plus in her type of business.

As Daniel strode down the narrow sidewalk toward the coffee shop's rear entrance, he heard what sounded like a scream cut short. It had come from across the street, toward the front of the building. Instinctively he cut around the coffee shop and sprinted toward the sound.

Dimly illuminated by the streetlight were two people lying on the grass between the sidewalk and the street curb, fighting. Reaching into his jacket pocket as he ran, Daniel brought out a small flashlight and switched it on.

A guy wearing a blue bandanna over his face, like a cheap rustler from an old cowboy movie, had a cord wrapped around a woman's neck. As the would-be killer turned his head to look, the glare of Daniel's beam blinded him for a heartbeat.

The suspect instinctively threw his arm up to shield his eyes, revealing Holly's face in the grass.

"Holly, roll!" he yelled, closing the gap between them.

Holly twisted away, breaking his grip. Her assailant im-

mediately jumped to his feet and swung around, crouched and
ready to counter Daniel's expected tackle.

Daniel led instead with a flying kick, catching the man
full force in the chest. The impact knocked his opponent off
the grass and across the narrow sidewalk, slamming his back
into the low stone wall that bordered the lawn of the residence
behind him. Daniel glanced at Holly, who was now on her
knees, coughing.

"I'm okay," she croaked, gasping for air.

Daniel focused once again on his enemy, who'd risen to his
feet and was now in a fighting stance, right leg and arm slightly
forward—his strong side.

"Come on," the man whispered harshly, motioning confi-
dently with his gloves. "Let's see what you've got."

His attacker clearly had some training, but Daniel knew the
initiative belonged to him now. He assumed an attack position,
hands up and open, ready to advance or kick, or block with his
forearms. The guy was bigger than he was, but that had never
been much of a problem.

The man advanced, throwing a left jab to set up a right.
Daniel slipped to the side, countering with a left punch to the
man's ribs as the incoming jab barely brushed his cheek. The
man gasped and rocked back, stunned by the blow.

Suddenly they were both illuminated by the headlights of
an approaching car. The glare caught Daniel by surprise and
he was forced to step back, arms up. Yet no blow came—his
attacker knew it was time to run.

Holly's assailant shot down the sidewalk, leaped the low
retaining wall, then raced across a front lawn toward a side
street.

"I'm going after him. Stay here," Daniel said, leaping over
the low wall.

Confident he could keep the man in sight and eventually
catch up to him, Daniel raced across the grass. As he started to
narrow the gap, the man faked left toward the street, then cut

right, heading down the side of the house toward a three-foot-high wall that enclosed the backyard. He jumped it cleanly, never breaking his stride.

Daniel followed seconds behind, but lost a step as he hurdled the wall and nearly collided with an outdoor grill. By then, his opponent was already nearing the opposite wall. Again, the man, wearing some kind of jogging sweats, hurdled the wall like a track star and actually gained ground.

Daniel reached the wall four seconds later and leaped over, only vaguely aware of the sound of a television program somewhere to his right.

As soon as he cleared the wall, he saw the back of the running man dodging some barren rosebushes as he sprinted toward another low wall on the far side of the next property.

Daniel knew he was gaining ground, but, focusing on his target, he nearly crashed into a rose trellis. He swerved at the last second, barely missing the plant. When he looked up, all he could see was the upper half of his target, fading away in the dark. The guy was a natural hurdler and soon went over the cinder block wall like an equestrian—minus the horse.

"Damn!" Daniel heard a female voice say from somewhere behind him and recognized Holly's voice. She'd followed. Why the hell were women so difficult? They always seemed to do the opposite of what a man expected.

He pushed back the distraction. At least she'd recovered quickly enough to race after them, so he didn't need to worry about her right now. He kept his gaze forward, and this time leaped just high enough to touch the wall with his right foot as he went over. It was easier now that he had his rhythm back, but he wasn't gaining enough to bring down the suspect.

The next yard had the back porch light on, and he could see his target clearly. Almost as if sensing that he wouldn't be able to outrun Daniel for long, the guy veered to his right, slipping on the cold grass and almost falling flat. Recovering quickly, he ducked around the side of the house toward the street and disappeared.

Daniel slowed down, suspecting a corner ambush, then caught a flash of something moving to his left, low to the ground. Spinning around, he saw a huge dog—or at least two rows of gleaming white teeth against a dark shape.

As the dog growled, Daniel jumped up onto the three foot wall. Forced to watch his feet, he ran along the narrow top. As soon as he reached the yard's wooden gate, he jumped high over the top, praying he wasn't leaping blind onto a stack of firewood.

Luck was with him. Daniel landed with a crunch on light gravel just as the dog slammed into the other side of the gate with an awesome thud.

Daniel glanced around quickly, but the driveway before him was empty. Then he heard the sound of squealing tires. As he turned his head back toward the boulevard, he saw taillights racing away. He'd lost him. It was over—for now.

He was walking back up the street in the direction of the coffee shop when he heard footsteps approaching to his right. "He's getting away," Holly called out, running across the lawn toward him. "I tried to catch up, but those danged walls kept slowing me down."

"I thought I told you to stay put."

Holly bristled. "And do what? Stand there gagging in the dark, hoping he wouldn't circle the block and come back for round two? I felt safer chasing *him*."

"Did you get the license plate, by any chance?"

"No, did you?" she answered.

He shook his head, dug his phone out of his pocket and dialed the police.

LESS THAN THREE minutes later, an officer drove up. The attractive blond officer recognized Daniel and smiled at him as she took out a small notebook. "You stirring up trouble on my beat again, Hawk?"

He gave her a grim smile. "It's good to see you, Penny," he said, then updated her, giving as much of a description as possible of their attacker.

"That's not much to go on. He's going to be changing his clothes right away, and his approximate height and build aren't going to give us much of a lead." Still taking notes, she glanced at Holly. "Did he speak to you at all, Ms. Gates?"

Holly shook her head. "No, he never said a word, Officer White," she said, noting the officer's name tag. "Somehow that made it even worse. He wanted me dead, but he had nothing to say to me?" Her voice broke at the last word and she swallowed hard.

"Have you had problems with anyone lately, an old boyfriend, maybe, or an ex-husband? A neighbor?"

Holly shook her head. "Never married, and no on the rest. Is there any attacker on the loose? Our neighborhood watch usually warns us regarding a crime spree, but I haven't heard about any serious problems lately."

"Things have been quiet," Officer White said. "Particularly in this neighborhood."

"Not anymore," Daniel said.

Officer White nodded somberly.

"I have one possible lead for you," Daniel said, then told her about the incident with Keeswood earlier that day.

"Clyde Keeswood's basically a loudmouth," Holly said, shaking her head. "He wants attention and makes noise to get it, but he's not really violent. He knew I'd see the chair coming and dodge. Had he really meant to hurt me, he would have rushed the podium."

"It's still possible that tonight's incident was in retaliation for what happened earlier," the officer said, placing her notebook back into her pocket. "We'll talk to Mr. Keeswood and get in touch with you if we need to do a follow-up. In the meantime, you might want to avoid going for walks alone at night," she said. Giving Daniel a quick nod and smile, Officer White got into her patrol car and drove off.

"Why don't we go have something to eat and try to sort this out? Are you up to it?" he asked, noticing how she had her arms folded, almost as if hugging herself.

She nodded, then walked with him up the street. "Do you really think this had something to do with my work for the tribe?"

"What happened tonight could have a dozen explanations, including a stalker, but let it go for now," he said, his voice steady. "Once you eat something and have a little time to relax, you may find that you're able to remember more, little details you might have blocked out because you were too busy staying alive."

"All right. I'll try. I want this man caught and put behind bars. He's…crazy."

"Maybe," Daniel muttered under his breath as he walked beside her down the sidewalk.

DANIEL ORDERED a green chile cheeseburger with the works. She decided on a grilled cheese sandwich. She wasn't at all hungry and her throat was a little sore, but from the looks of it, Daniel had worked up quite an appetite after tonight's run.

Holly picked at her sandwich and sipped the warm, soothing chamomile-and-peppermint-flavored tea, one of her favorites. Logic told her that it was over and she had nothing else to fear, but she still couldn't quite make herself relax.

"You saved my life tonight and I haven't even thanked you yet," she said, warming her hands on the ceramic mug she was holding.

He smiled. "It's not necessary, but I'd like you to answer one question for me. You were unarmed, yet you still raced after the man who tried to strangle you. What were you planning to do if you caught him?"

"I can't fight, but I might have been able to distract him while you did the rough stuff," she said, then paused before continuing, "There are many ways to win a fight, Daniel. Sometimes it's a matter of buying someone else a few seconds to act."

"You're right," he said. "Diversions can be crucial in some situations."

"Earlier today, you offered to give me some pointers on how to spot trouble. I'm ready to listen. The guy walked right up to me and I never thought a thing about it until he grabbed me by the shoulders. By then it was too late."

He nodded. "All right. For starters, when you're giving a talk, watch individuals, not just the overall group. Look for behavior that doesn't fit in with the others present. Search for small telltale signs, not just confrontational stares. For example, people who are lying or have an agenda tend to touch their face a lot. If you're close enough, watch for downward gazes, too, or looking off to the right. Attitude and posturing are the keys. Guys looking for trouble often telegraph their intentions," he said. "The single most important thing is this—if you think there's going to be trouble, get backup fast."

"No problem there. I'm not a fighter by nature," she said quietly.

"You're still scared, aren't you?" he asked softly. "You don't have to be. He's gone. He got a lot more than he bargained for tonight."

"Yes, but will he come back and try again? Not knowing is the worst part of this." She wished she could have said something tough and brave sounding instead, but the truth was that she was terrified. "I wish you'd have just brought out your gun and held him until the police came, instead of fighting him face-to-face."

"It's locked up in my SUV. I rarely carry it off the job. Besides, I never draw my weapon unless I'm going to use it and that wasn't an option tonight. I never had a clear line of fire."

He took a deep breath. "Guns aren't always the best solution, either. A show of deadly force often provokes a lethal response from your opponent, and stray bullets don't discriminate. When I draw my weapon, it's because I have no other choice, and the person who forced that response is likely to end up dead."

The total lack of emotion in his voice chilled her to the bone. Yet the way his hand had curled into a hard fist revealed another story. Beyond his acceptance of the inevitability of violence was an acute awareness of the cost it exacted.

"My job is very different from yours," she said with a soft sigh. "It's about logic, and reason, and the ability to communicate effectively. The incident with the chair this morning isn't the norm at all. Mind you, cranks and protesters will shout all kinds of things, but until today, I've never had that escalate into an actual physical attack."

"The problem is that the *Diné* have been lied to for centuries, and the tribe is still paying the price for believing outsiders—illnesses and death from unsafe mining operations, contaminated water and ground poisoned by uranium."

"But this is the tribe's own process. No one's lying to anyone."

"You see tribal government working on behalf of its people, but *Diné* activists see Anglo corporations coming to talk to our leaders and selling them a bill of goods. You're going to keep having problems," Daniel said. "The protesters are going on the offensive, so you need to stay alert whenever you're in public."

"And know when to duck?"

He chuckled. "Yeah, that, too."

As they talked, Holly found herself relaxing and enjoying Daniel's company. After they finished dessert, she once again tried to review the details of what had happened earlier. Though she worked hard to look at the events objectively, no new answers came to her.

"What happened to me tonight…it must have been random.

In my business I don't make these types of enemies. I'm a spokesperson, that's all, not someone who implements policy. The man who came at me must have had his own agenda."

"You might be right," he said, but his tone said he was unconvinced.

"It's getting late," she said, glancing at the clock on the wall. "I don't want to walk back home alone. Would you give me a ride?"

"Be glad to."

They left the coffee shop and rode back in his SUV. The interior was spotless and smelled of leather and lime aftershave. She sat back, glad for the company, particularly now. There was something very reassuring about Daniel's presence.

When they pulled up in front of her home a short time later, she saw him studying her front porch, watching the white swing that swayed gently in the cool breeze.

"I'd invite you in, but I need to try and get some sleep. I've got an early meeting tomorrow," she said.

"My guess is that you still have too much adrenaline pumping through your system. I know—I've been there. What's your way of relaxing? Music, exercise or something else?"

It was the way he'd emphasized those last two words that immediately sparked her imagination. She could have sworn she'd heard a very tempting invitation there.

Holly pushed the thought aside. She wasn't thinking clearly, that's all. The man had asked her a simple question.

"I'm going to go inside, put on my fuzzy slippers and break open the box of chocolate truffles I've been saving for my next celebration."

"Celebration? Tonight? What's the occasion?"

"I survived. It doesn't get much better than that."

Not giving him a chance to answer, she climbed out of his SUV, waved goodbye and walked to the front porch.

Chapter Four

As the owner of TechTalk Incorporated, Holly was her own boss, but she still had to answer to her clients. Martin Roanhorse wasn't as difficult as most, but he could be demanding, particularly when things weren't flowing as smoothly as he wanted. Right now, from the look on his face, she could tell that something had upset him.

"I heard about the incident last night," he said as she took the seat he offered. "You shouldn't have been wandering around alone outside, particularly after what happened here yesterday."

Since it was barely eight in the morning, she was surprised to find out he already knew of the attack. "I was on my way to meet someone," she said calmly. "In case you're worried, I don't think it had anything to do with my job." She paused then added, "How did you find out so quickly?"

"I spoke to Daniel Hawk this morning."

She blinked. "He's already here?"

He nodded. "Down the hall. He's going over a scheduled training op with our security team. The briefing started at daybreak," he said, then quickly got back to the matter at hand. "Have you heard anything from the Hartley police?"

"No, not yet."

"Your work is important to the tribe, Holly, so I'm authorized to provide you with protection if you think it might be necessary. Just say the word," he said.

Martin's offer caught her off guard. She'd worked all night to convince herself that what had happened was the result of an unlucky set of circumstances, nothing more. Having to once again face the possibility that she might continue to be a target made a cold shiver race up her spine.

She took a breath, trying to calm herself down. Forcing all doubts and fear from her voice, she answered Martin. "Thank you very much, but that's not necessary. I really think it was an isolated thing."

"But you can't be sure," he said, voicing the thought that whispered from the dark corners of her mind. "Let's keep the offer on the table for now, just in case."

She started to argue, then stopped. Creating problems or encouraging needless confrontations wasn't her style.

"When you called this meeting, you mentioned that you had a new assignment for me," she said, bringing him back to the business at hand.

Martin nodded. "Some of our investors are still concerned that this facility will be vulnerable to sabotage, especially after it became clear that our new exploration and recovery operations are being challenged. So I'd like you to go meet Daniel Hawk and observe today's special training exercise. A team of ex-police officers acting as terrorists will mount an assault and our own security people will have to counter it. It's meant to test the effectiveness of the protective measures we have in place. Afterward, I'd like you to present our investors with the results of the exercise, which I believe will be positive. Just don't give out details of the actual tactics we use here. Those have to remain classified."

"Is the exercise going to include this building?" she asked.

"No, that would disrupt other business. The target is the new building behind this one, which is still just a shell at the moment. Arthur Larrabee will be directing the assault team. Do you know him?"

"The name sounds familiar…" she said, trying to place it.

"He's running for city council over in Hartley."

She smiled and nodded. "Now I remember. He started campaigning early. Elections are six months from now."

"Larrabee's an ex-police officer who also teaches police science classes at the college. We needed someone who could seriously challenge Daniel Hawk's strategies and tactics, and that was tough to find. Most of the top people in that field are already at work in other facilities."

"Hawk—he's that good?"

"You better believe it," he said without hesitation. "Larrabee's his equal, though—at least on paper."

"Better at the job?"

"No, not better," Roanhorse said slowly. "Their methods are different, that's all. Larrabee's strategy is to deploy large, heavily armed security forces. Hawk…" His voice trailed off as he thought about it. "Hawk's tactics call for small, highly trained teams."

"Size doesn't always matter," a familiar voice said from behind Holly. As she turned, Daniel smiled and entered the office. "A handful of highly trained experts can block access to the most vulnerable targets and neutralize any intruders."

"That sounds logical," Holly said.

"Larrabee hasn't made his move yet, but everything's in place," Daniel said.

"Then take Ms. Gates with you and brief her, Daniel," Martin said. "Make sure she knows what parts of the operation need to remain secret."

"Roger that."

Daniel led the way out of Martin's office and walked with Holly down the hall. "My observation post is at the far end of this building. We've got an extensive camera network there that will help me monitor each phase of the exercise."

She followed him into a small office and saw a myriad of screens mounted on shelves. He pointed to the only seat, an office chair on casters. "Go ahead, sit. I prefer to stand."

She took the chair. "Can you give me a rundown on what you expect to take place?"

"No time. It's starting," he said, pointing to one of the screens as he adjusted his small headset. "Vibration detectors in the ground have picked up footsteps outside the back fence. Those men at the front gate are probably only a diversion meant to misdirect our security officers." He used the mouse to open a second view of three other, armed men scaling the perimeter fence with a ladder.

"They have guns. I thought this was only a drill," Holly said quickly.

"It is. Everyone's wearing sensors, and those tubes on the barrels are lasers. They'll be shooting light, not bullets."

"Like laser tag."

"Pretty much." He checked the other screens and saw two men approaching a camera alongside the key building. One stood on the other's shoulder and placed a piece of tape over the lens. Immediately another camera across the compound focused on the act, covering and recording it. Next, one of the men brought out a handful of keys and began trying them on the lock.

"The bad guys wouldn't have keys, would they? Wouldn't they just blow the door?" Holly asked.

"Yeah, but we can't afford to keep buying new doors and locks just for a training op. The amount of time needed to find the right key is a variable, just like the time it takes to place the explosives."

There was a tone that came over a speaker, and the man covering the one with the keys turned around, shaking his head.

Holly saw a small device strapped to his chest, now blinking. "He's been shot, right?" Holly asked.

There was another beep. The one with the keys turned around, mouthing an easy to recognize curse. "Yeah, and we just got the other one, too. Snipers are covering the building exteriors and the walkways between structures. Our tactics funnel any assaulting personnel into capture or kill zones."

"What about those men out front, creating the diversion?" Holly looked back at the front gate.

"They're locked out. Another gate will swing shut if they somehow get past the first team of guards. There's also a metal plate in the road that'll keep anyone from crashing through in a vehicle."

"What if somebody comes over or under the fence and is unarmed? If you're dealing with a zealot or someone who's disturbed, will they get shot, too?"

Daniel shook his head. "If we don't see firearms or suspicious packages, then the guards use Tasers, gas or rubber bullets—normally nonlethal weapons."

Ten minutes later, Daniel's phone rang. He spoke for a moment, hung up and looked at Holly.

"Every intruder has been neutralized. They didn't get inside the building," Daniel said, smiling. "Larrabee's going to be spitting mad. You'll meet him soon. He'll be coming in to debrief. Now that he knows where the cameras are, he'll be asked to mount another exercise in a few days. Meanwhile, our security people will meet and work out any potential weaknesses in our tactics. I don't play a more active role because this is *their* test."

"I'll leave you to it, then. I'll pitch this as exacting security measures that anticipate trouble and protect against all manner of intrusions. Sound good?"

"Yeah, that's precisely what it is."

As he stepped forward to hang his headset on a hook, she stood and their chests touched. Her skin prickled, but she stopped short of sucking in her breath.

"Sorry. It's a tight fit," he said, stepping back but bumping into the desk.

"Which is why I'm leaving," she said, turning just as a dark-haired Anglo man wearing a desert camouflage suit, boonie hat and leaf-green camo-creme face paint appeared at the door.

"Larrabee," Daniel said, nodding.

"You've got observers?" Larrabee said, standing in the doorway.

"I'm Holly Gates for TTI. The tribe's corporate partners wanted some additional information on security measures here," she said. "I've got what I need now, so I'll be on my way."

"Don't rush off, pretty lady," Larrabee said, giving her a wink.

"We've got a debrief to take care of right now, Art," Daniel said. "Let's not get distracted."

Roanhorse came up behind Larrabee just then. "Sorry to interrupt, gentlemen, but I need to see both of you in my office."

Daniel motioned Larrabee to the door, then followed him out.

Holly was the last to leave the room. She closed the door behind her, then stopped by the water cooler as the others continued down the hall. If she'd read Martin's expression right, there was a new problem brewing. She had a feeling she'd find out what it was before she left this morning.

In the interim, there was another person she wanted to see. She walked down the hall in the opposite direction.

As she entered the last doorway to her left, Jane Begay looked up and smiled. Jane was a beautiful Navajo woman with long black hair, normally fastened at the nape of her neck while at work. Today, she wore a nondescript brown wool pantsuit with a plain white turtleneck sweater beneath, but what set it off was the beautiful turquoise-and-silver squash blossom necklace around her neck.

"It's good to see you, safe and sound. I heard that you've been having all kinds of trouble lately," Jane said, offering Holly a seat.

She and Jane were good friends. She'd been the one who'd

recommended Holly for the job here at the new natural gas processing plant. Jane served as the local IT person, maintaining the computer network and training employees to use their specialized software and electronic systems.

Briefly, Holly explained what had happened the night before. "Years ago, this kind of attack would have been unheard of in the Four Corners, but now...."

"Yeah, progress," Jane said in a hushed tone. "Are you being extra careful?"

"I'll be looking over my shoulder a lot more, sure," Holly admitted, "but I refuse to hide in my closet and cower."

"I hear you," Jane said, "but don't let pride or bluster get in the way of common sense. I know you like your independence, but you might need a little extra help right now."

She had a feeling Jane already knew about Martin's offer of protection. "Maybe the guy isn't after me specifically. It could be that he was out looking for a victim, and there I was."

"You can't be sure of that," Jane said, then lowered her voice to a conspiratorial tone. "I just came out of a top-level meeting. The tribe is considering requiring you to accept protection, at least for a while."

"If anything else happens, I'll accept, but I think it's too early to make that decision." Holly paused then added, "Do you know if they have anyone in particular in mind as my bodyguard?"

"At first they considered Arthur Larrabee—the ex-policeman. He works for us on a contract basis, and could have fit it into his schedule. He also has the skills to keep you safe, but he's been taken off the list."

"Why?" Holly was curious, but not unhappy.

"This is all off the record. You'll keep it confidential?"

Holly nodded. "Sure."

"Arthur's former girlfriend, Megan Olson, has disappeared, at least according to her relatives. Arthur and Megan dated for a while, then recently split up. There's nothing to indicate that Arthur's got anything to do with her disappearance, but Arthur's a person of interest because he was supposedly one of the last people to see her," she said. "Her family's influential and they're demanding answers. It's just politics, but Martin has decided not to renew Arthur's contract with us. He doesn't want any negative publicity spilling over onto us, not right now."

"That explains why Martin didn't press me harder to accept the offer of protection this morning. He normally doesn't give up so easily."

"Your real problem is that you're too independent. You don't want anyone telling you what to do and when."

"Am I that transparent?" Holly asked with a rueful smile. "No, don't answer that."

"Regardless of what you want, if there's another incident, the tribe will insist that you accept their offer of protection. We need you right now. My advice is don't fight it."

"Nothing else is going to happen," Holly said, hoping that was true, and stood. "Right now, I need to get some materials ready for the upcoming job fair in Hartley. The plant is ready to hire additional staff to work here and out in the field. I've also got to study my notes and get another presentation ready for a new group of investors." Holly checked her watch. "Time for me to head over to my office in Hartley."

Chapter Five

Holly was soon on her way, driving down the long graveled road toward the main highway. As the road stretched out her thoughts drifted to Daniel. He seemed like a force of nature, always active, even in stillness. He clearly didn't take challenges lightly, either.

She'd seen the spark of competitiveness in his eyes when Larrabee had entered the room. Of course Larrabee had more than his share of *machismo,* and even in nature, alpha males clashed. Some things were just hardwired into the species.

Holly was halfway to the highway when she saw the fast rising plume of sand and dust behind her. Her skin prickled even as she told herself to relax. She wasn't likely to be the only human being leaving the plant, even between shifts. Someone was just in a hurry to reach the highway. She couldn't afford to overreact every time she saw a person traveling in the same direction she was.

Realizing how isolated she was out here, she decided to play it safe. Holly took the next right, moving toward a new Rez housing area. She'd expected the vehicle behind her to continue directly to the highway, but it took the same turn she did and continued following at a distance.

Holly made a few more random, last minute turns down residential streets where there were more homes than vacant lots, but the vehicle remained on her tail, taking the same turns.

Her heart began beating overtime. There was no way she

could go to her office in Hartley now and lead whoever was back there right to her door.

Holly tried hard not to give in to panic, but the possibility that this was the same guy who'd attacked her at the coffee shop was terrifying. What if he already knew where her office was, or where she lived?

She pushed back her fears, forcing herself to think clearly. If this *was* the same guy, she needed to get a description without further endangering herself. She considered pulling over as soon as she rounded the next curve in the road and waiting for him to pass, but then changed her mind. That was too risky. If he was really stalking her, he'd likely stop, as well, and then what, shoot her? Trying to force the other driver into making any kind of move at all wasn't a good idea, and if she headed back to the plant, any hope of catching him would fade away. He'd be stupid to follow.

Then it came to her. What she needed was backup. The tribal police department was badly undermanned, and getting a patrol cruiser to her location could take hours. There was only one other logical option. Holly used her Bluetooth and called Daniel. He answered a moment later and Holly quickly told him where she was and what was happening.

"Keep driving through that residential area and stay on the phone. I'll be there in a few minutes to back you up. If he closes in, find a house where you think someone's home and run for the door."

"All right." As Holly continued circling, the other driver stayed with her.

"He's still there and keeps his distance whether I speed up or slow down," Holly said, trying to keep her voice from cracking. "He knows I've spotted him. Why doesn't he take off?"

"Get back on the plant road so I can catch up to you sooner. I'm not too far from your current location, maybe three minutes. Once I have you in sight I'll let you know. Keep the phone line open."

Three minutes later, Holly spoke again. "I've turned onto the plant road, heading north toward the highway. I'm about a quarter mile from the three-way intersection before the big arroyo, the one with the irrigation ditches on either side. There aren't any other vehicles around except for the guy following me. The oncoming lane is clear."

"I'm at the top of the hill and can see you now," Daniel said. "Here's what I want you to do."

Following his directions precisely, Holly sped up, then, just before the intersection, swerved into the incoming lane. Braking at the last possible second, she cut to the right and slid in the gravel, blocking the road.

Her heart was beating overtime as she looked over her right shoulder and saw the oncoming sedan. He'd have to leave the road and drop into the ditch to get around her now. Or ram—

"Stay in the car," Daniel said, almost as if reading her mind. "I've got him."

The driver following her slowed. She could see him behind the wheel now, but he had a cap low over his eyes, and sunglasses. As he headed straight for her, her mouth went completely dry and her heart began to pound. Slowly, he veered to his right, apparently hoping to slip around the front of her truck.

Holly let off the clutch and inched her pickup forward to close the gap. Ducking down, she gripped the steering wheel hard. If he crashed into her, her air bags would deploy and those, she prayed, would keep her from getting hurt.

Holly heard sliding tires, flying gravel, and braced herself. There was a thump and rumble, but the crash never came. As she peered up Holly saw the sedan flash by in her rearview mirror.

The guy had faked her out, cutting behind her pickup and

dropping a tire into the ditch. His car fishtailed, gravel flew, then picked up speed again.

"He got past me, Daniel," she said, speaking into her Blue-tooth. "I can back around and try—"

"No. Just get out of your truck. When I come by, jump in and we'll go after him together," Daniel said.

Holly climbed out, keys and phone in hand, and waited as Daniel eased past her truck. When he slid to a stop in the middle of the road, she raced over and jumped into his SUV.

"Seat belt," Daniel ordered, already on the move as she reached for the buckle. Once he heard the click of the buckle, he pressed down on the gas pedal and the force threw her back into the seat.

They were hundreds of yards behind the man now, but the terrain was pretty flat and he was still within sight.

"I called the tribal P.D. as I was running for the SUV. With luck, they'll have a roadblock set up along the highway," he said, giving her a quick once-over. "You okay?"

"Yeah. All I have to do now is stop shaking," she said with a quick smile.

"You're doing fine. You kept your cool and are safe. Now let's go catch him."

Daniel's SUV slid around a corner at high speed, but re-mained in control. Although the car ahead was raising dust like never before, they were still gaining ground.

"He's not headed for the highway anymore," Holly said. "That road just circles back to the housing development."

"Yeah, I know. Hang on."

They closed to within a hundred yards, then suddenly the sedan ahead hit its brakes, swerved and slid onto a narrow irrigation ditch road. On one side was a steep drop to a fence line, and beyond, a fallow field. Opposite it was a deep but empty irrigation ditch.

"Why take the ditch road?" Holly asked. "If he goes any faster now, he'll lose control and maybe flip the car."

"I've never gone this way. Do you know where it leads?" Daniel asked, concentrating on his driving. The dirt road was narrow and bumpy, and if he hit a big rock or a fallen branch, they'd wreck for sure.

"It makes a ninety-degree turn up ahead, intersects the highway, then picks up again on the other side," she said. "There's a culvert underneath the road."

"He's likely to be T-boned if he tries to cross the highway."

"Or take out some innocent driver. He's going as fast as he can," she said.

"Yeah, good point. I'd better slow down. Maybe he'll back off the accelerator, too, if we stop closing the gap. We can't risk getting somebody killed," Daniel said, looking over at her as he took his foot off the gas pedal. "Damn. Wish I had a siren."

Holly nodded.

The highway was just ahead, and through gaps in the trees lining the road, she could see cars racing past, unaware of the oncoming danger.

Gripping her seat, her eyes fixed ahead, Holly saw the driver hit his brakes at the last second, slide sideways and lean on the horn. The sedan slid out into the asphalt, all the way into the inside lane.

The loud squeal of brakes rose into the air as a big delivery truck skidded into view from the left. Blue smoke from hot rubber and screaming brakes flew everywhere like a cloud. The truck slid sideways, then slowly tipped over onto the passenger side and slid another hundred feet. Sparks flew like fireworks as metal raked the asphalt.

Daniel braked to a stop, skidding but still maintaining control. Cars to their left slammed their brakes, fighting to slow down to avoid hitting the truck.

Holly looked down the road to her right and watched the man who'd come after her disappear to the east. "Luck always seems to be on his side," she said in a shaky whisper.

Daniel jumped out of the SUV, then, noting that the oncoming traffic had come to a stop, raced over to the delivery truck and helped the driver open his door, like a hatch, and climb out.

Another driver had parked his pickup, flashers on, and was already trying to guide traffic around the blocked lane. Holly escorted the man from the wrecked truck to the side of the road, then waited as he contacted his employer.

Soon the wail of a siren rose in the distance and Holly could see flashing emergency lights coming from the west, in the direction of the reservation town of Shiprock. While she was watching Daniel and the other driver direct traffic, her cell phone rang.

"What's going on?" Martin Roanhorse asked. "I heard someone was tailing you."

She updated him as she watched a white tribal police department SUV weave its way around stopped cars and over to the scene. "Whoever was following me is long gone," Holly added, "and his license plate was covered, maybe with tape. It's a dead end."

"That settles it. I want you and Daniel back in my office as soon as you're free."

Holly hung up and slipped the phone back into her jacket pocket. Her hands were still shaking, but her fear was slowly giving way to anger. She'd never purposely harmed anyone in her life, yet for some unfathomable reason, a very crazy person was coming after her. If he was hoping she'd panic and do something stupid he was in for a surprise. This wasn't her kind of battle, but she was a fast learner.

Her gaze drifted to Daniel, who was talking to a uniformed Navajo officer. Soon the officer nodded, and Daniel came over to join her.

"I just got a call from Martin," Holly said. "He wants to see both of us."

"Ready when you are."

As they drove back to the plant, Daniel glanced over at her.

"Martin can be hard-nosed about security matters. Don't be surprised if he downgrades your clearance until this matter is settled."

Surprised, she stared back at Daniel. What he'd said was logical, but until now, she hadn't even considered that disastrous possibility. If Martin restricted her access, she'd be unable to continue her work at the facility. In essence, she'd lose the account, and at the worst possible time. Every cent she had was tied into her fledgling company. She couldn't afford to forfeit a contract.

She'd been worried about being forced to accept protection, but that no longer seemed like such a bad alternative. Holly took a deep breath. Part of her job entailed persuading people to open their minds, and that's exactly what she'd have to do now. Her livelihood depended on it.

Chapter Six

Daniel dropped Holly off in Martin's office. "I've got something I need to do. I'll catch up to you in a few minutes."

She nodded, her eyes still on Martin, who was finishing a phone conversation. "I'll be here."

He watched her a moment longer. The incident had rattled her more than she'd admitted, but he had no time to dwell on that now. While still at the accident scene he'd received a call from his brother, Detective Preston Bowman of the Hartley Police Department.

He'd known all along that his brother would eventually investigate the incident with Holly since it had happened on his beat. So when Preston had insisted they meet for coffee at the plant, he hadn't hesitated.

As Daniel went into his office, he saw his brother was already there.

"You made good time," Daniel said.

"I had a meeting at the tribal police station. I was in the area." Preston gave his brother a long, thorough inspection. "You look beat."

"No, just angry."

"I received the report detailing the assault on Holly Gates." Preston studied his brother with a laser-sharp gaze. "Be careful, Dan, you can't just jump in every time somebody needs to be rescued."

"This is just business."

"You sure? From what I've already heard here and there, she's a looker."

Daniel refused to make eye contact. He hated the way Preston could read him so easily.

"The woman works here. I'm just lending a hand."

"Yeah, yeah. Sell that to someone who doesn't know you." Preston sat on one of the chairs and waited.

"So what did you want to see me about?" Daniel asked, refusing to sit. He stared at a painting of Shiprock on the wall, wishing he had a window to distract him.

"Just wanted to know how things are going. Gene's staying at your place?"

"Yeah, for now. I'm glad he took the job of taking care of the paperwork associated with *Hosteen* Silver's trust. The old man had nothing except for the house and cabin, but there are still a million things that need to be handled."

"Yeah, I hear you. Paperwork—it's never ending." He paused for a long time, then stood and walked over, putting his hand on Daniel's shoulder. "We need to get this woman out of your head for a minute and talk family."

"She's not in—" Daniel said, looked at Preston, then shrugged. "Okay, yeah, maybe a little."

"Gene told me about the note *Hosteen* Silver left in the safe-deposit box. I thought those final request letters *Hosteen* Silver left each of us would be it, but obviously I was wrong," Preston said, taking a seat again. "Do you still have a copy of the note?"

"Yeah. The original's still in the box. Have a look," Daniel said, then pulled it out of his pocket. "I'd like your take on this."

"This is the story about Changing Bear Maiden, Coyote's wife, but there's a question mark over the entire text," Preston said. "That doesn't make any sense. Why save and protect such a well-known account, and more importantly, why the question mark? To *Hosteen* Silver these weren't legends—they were a way of explaining the world. Everything had its purpose."

"I think he was trying to send us a message, something he wasn't quite sure about, that only we should see. Unfortunately, I'm drawing a blank," Daniel said.

"Me, too," Preston said at last, handing it back.

"It was left there for a reason," Daniel said.

Preston nodded. "I agree. We'll have a family meeting once everyone's home and figure it out together. In the meantime, keep thinking." Preston walked to Daniel's coffeepot and found it empty. "What's a guy gotta do to get a cup of coffee around here?"

Daniel reached for the doorknob and cocked his head. "Come on."

They walked down the hall, side by side, then Preston poked Daniel in the ribs. "Can't wait to meet this Holly woman, Dan. She's got you all turned around inside."

"Yeah, right," Daniel muttered as they approached the small coffee bar at the cafeteria.

Preston shot his brother a look and chuckled. "Oh, yeah. You're going down, bro."

HOLLY SAT IN Martin's office, searching her mind for a way to convince him. The fixed look on his face told her she had her work cut out for her.

"Your problem is a lot bigger than I originally thought," Martin said. "The person after you is persistent enough to pursue you in broad daylight. That could end up affecting security here at this facility."

"Nobody can say for certain that today's incident was related to what happened outside the café last night," Holly said. "More important, it didn't happen *here*."

"I'd like you to consider taking a leave of absence. We need your services, but not if there's any chance that you pose a risk to operations at this plant."

"You offered me protection this morning," Holly said, looking over at Daniel, who'd come in just moments ago. "Is that still on the table?"

Martin nodded slowly.

"Then let me take you up on that now. In addition, I'll ask the security officer to teach me how to defend myself," she said, but, out of the corner of her eye, saw Daniel shake his head. "Also, I'll have them recommend locks and safety devices I can use in my home and car."

"Forget the self-defense lessons. You can't fight this type of assailant on your own," Daniel said, his voice calm. "You'd need months of training to be able to neutralize his size, strength and height advantage—not to mention experience."

"I'm not advocating a long, drawn-out, hand-to-hand battle. All I'd need to do is break loose so I can get help," Holly said.

"You won't need combat training if you have security with you at all times, but I like the rest of what you proposed," Martin said. "It's a done deal."

She breathed a silent sigh of relief. At least she still had a job.

"Security is meant to keep you safe, not restrict your work. It'll be easier on you if you remember that," Martin said, leaning back in his chair and regarding her for a long moment.

"I will," Holly answered. "And I really appreciate what you're doing."

"As I've said before, we need your help here. You deal with the demands of our culture as easily as you do your own. You remember that we don't shake hands, and in fact, we dislike touching strangers. When you're speaking to our traditionalist elders, you show respect by not using their proper names. You avoid direct eye contact and you don't press for quick answers. Most important of all, our investors come from all over the world, and you honor both their ways and ours by maintaining harmony. By protecting you, we're helping restore the balance that helps all of us walk in beauty."

"It's good to hear that my work's appreciated. Thank you very much," she said.

"As of right now, I'm assigning Daniel to you," Martin said. "He's our best."

"Just so I'm clear," she said. "This is only a temporary arrangement until the police catch this lunatic, right?"

"Of course," Martin said. "Once the threat is gone we can return to our standard on-site security protocols."

For Martin, it had been purely a business decision, and she had to admit it made sense. Yet having Daniel as her bodyguard posed a danger all its own. He was high-voltage excitement, a walking temptation to anyone still drawing breath.

She nodded, knowing Martin was watching her reaction. "Okay, then. Daniel is familiar with the situation so he and I will work things out together."

Martin looked at each of them and nodded. "Good."

As they walked out of Martin's office, Daniel glanced over at her. "You made a smart decision. You're not on a level playing field with the guy who's after you. He's come at you using two different M.O.s, and he's shown that he's not afraid to put himself at risk."

"As much as I hate to admit it, he really scares me. Of course that's exactly what he wants, since it gives him a psychological advantage."

"Take that away from him by considering the odds. He's outnumbered now—by a wide margin. There are three law enforcement agencies looking for him, so it's only a matter of time before he's behind bars."

"In the meantime, I'll also have to figure out a way to protect my company so it won't take a hit. Being able to set people at ease is a big part of my business. That's going to be hard to do if word of this gets out, or people see I need a bodyguard."

"Think of it this way. I'm your deterrent. I'll keep trouble at bay—for you and your business."

"I know, and I'm grateful," she answered with an apologetic

smile. "It's waiting around for something to happen that's going to drive me crazy."

"I'm not good at that, either. I prefer to be proactive."

"Good, then why don't we team up and push to find answers on our own?"

"I was told to protect you, not do police work," he said.

"But to protect me effectively, you'll need to do both, don't you think? We have to anticipate problems, like you do in your training exercises, and stay ahead of the game. It's better to force this guy out into the open on our terms than to meet him on his."

He considered it for a moment, then finally nodded as they reached his SUV. "I'll tell you what. Let me drive you to wherever you need to go next, and we'll talk more about this on the way."

"I was going to ask you to take me to where I left my truck."

He shook his head. "I'll have someone I trust pick it up and park it in here inside the fence."

"Here are the keys, then. Take them to whoever you want, then we can head over to my office in Hartley."

A few minutes later as they drove down the highway, she took the opportunity to evaluate Daniel from a new perspective—as *her* private security. The determined set of his jaw and the way his strong hands gripped the wheel were reassuring details.

Yet there was no way she could ever let her guard down around him. That smile, those broad shoulders, that world-class butt, all sparked her imagination and left her yearning for things that were too dangerous to contemplate. To make matters worse, though she was very good at reading people, she couldn't even begin to figure out what Daniel was thinking.

"If I agree to help you track down the guy who's after you, it'll have to be under my terms. When I tell you to do something—do it. No arguments."

His tone of voice made her bristle. "I stink at taking orders, but I'm happy to listen to requests or suggestions."

"Then the deal's off."

"Whoa! You're not much for negotiations, are you?"

"Not on something like this. You have your areas of expertise—I have mine. I'll keep both of us alive, but only if you do what I say and trust my judgment all the way."

"All right," Holly said after a beat. "When it comes to security, you take the lead. But when we're talking to people, let me handle it, okay? We have no legal standing or leverage, so logic and persuasion are the best tools we've got."

"What makes you think you're better at that than I am?"

"It's what I do every day. I deal with tough issues, and when I'm faced with opposition, my job is to reach people by using reason and common sense."

Daniel considered it, then nodded. "All right. We'll see how that plays out." He stopped for a traffic light, the first on the western outskirts of the town, then continued when the light changed. "Before we left, I spoke to Preston Bowman, the detective in charge of the case. He told me that they've already spoken to Clyde Keeswood, but turned up nothing."

"Like I said before, I don't think Keeswood's our guy. There's something else going on here, some other motive for all that has happened. What I'm hoping, is that this…stalker… will find out we're tracking *him*. Then maybe he'll make a mistake. If we can figure out who he is, we can turn him over to the police."

"Just be aware of the risk. You can't start questioning people without endangering yourself," he warned. "The closer we get, the more likely he is to predict *our* next moves."

"I'm already facing a life-or-death situation. Degrees don't matter that much."

"Okay, so now we need a list of people to interview. Start thinking of anyone you've had disagreements with, maybe a guy you cut off in traffic, or a neighbor who gives you problems. Look at your professional contacts, too, like maybe a person you didn't recommend for a job, or beat out of an account. It doesn't take much to anger someone who's a little off-kilter already."

She nodded, then took out a small notebook she kept in her purse. For several moments she stared at the blank page. "This is really hard."

"That's because you're thinking of it as a list of suspects," he said, pulling into the parking lot of the small, one-story building she'd given him as her office address. "Start by listing people you work with or encounter on a daily basis—anyone— friends, casual acquaintances or even people you meet in the hall regularly. Once you have something on paper, then you can start crossing out the ones who seem less likely to either be the man we're looking for, or someone associated with him."

"In a way, I hope it's no one I can think of, because I can't think of anything worse than being betrayed by a friend."

Chapter Seven

A short time later Holly led the way inside her office. The interior was small and simple, and as she glanced at him she wondered what he thought of it. "It's not fancy, but it's quiet and has great high-speed internet. Most of my meetings take place at my clients' offices. They're usually more at ease in their own environment."

Holly stopped by her desk, which was at the center of the room. "This is my pride and joy," she said. "I bought it when the old Hartley Hotel on Butler Street was scheduled for demolition." Although small, the front and side panels were intricately carved. The heavy, handcrafted antique had caught her eye instantly, and she'd been lucky enough to bring in the winning bid.

"Despite years of neglect, some of the furnishings up for sale were salvageable once I stripped off layers of old, flaked varnish and paint," she said. "I bought the desk, some chairs and even the wooden file cabinets over there against the wall."

He nodded, but when he didn't say anything, she continued, "Am I talking too much? I tend to do that when I'm nervous. I'm boring you, right?"

"No, not at all," he said, looking around at the framed oils on the walls depicting Southwestern landscapes. "I gather that you either can't afford to pass up a good deal, or you don't like to see waste."

"Both," she admitted.

"Your office looks…comfortable," he said at last, his gaze

taking in the two matching barrel-style oak armchairs with black leather upholstery. "I like it a lot more than I do Martin's office, I can tell you that."

She laughed. "His office is intended to remind his visitors that he's a man of importance."

"But you don't want to be seen in the same light?"

"Our jobs are different. I don't need to assert authority as much as I have to demonstrate competence. When I do have a client here the first thing I try to do is convince them that I can be an asset to their company. It's not about how important I am, it's about what I can do for them."

"Tell me more about your work," he said, taking a seat in the closest armchair.

She leaned back against her desk and faced him. "Most of the time I'm hired to help corporations sell themselves, not just their projects. The Four Corners, historically, has had so many disasters that it's hard to earn the public's trust."

"What do you do when you meet protesters with closed minds?"

"I try to keep in mind that their reactions are usually based on fear. They've learned the hard way that you can't trust words. So I stick to the facts and present them as clearly and simply as possible."

"And if that doesn't work?"

"Then I have to work around them. People like Keeswood belong to a different generation. They believed the ones who told them that the uranium tailings piled around the mines on the Rez were safe. The *Diné* paid a very high price for those lies. The mining companies eventually shut down, declared bankruptcy and moved on. The tribe was left to knit the broken pieces of their lives back together again. Now, as a result, many of them automatically oppose any form of industry. For them, trust isn't an option."

"So, basically, the protesters see you as their enemy," Daniel concluded.

"Sometimes, but even Keeswood knows that I believe what I'm saying. He's just afraid that I'm being duped, too."

"What if he wanted to make you an example, a kill the messenger type of thing?"

"I really have a problem believing that. Clyde Keeswood is fighting to make sure the past is never repeated. He's trying to save lives, not take them. He hates what he sees as a new threat to The People, not me personally. I don't hate him, I don't even dislike him. He's got plenty of reasons for being the way he is, and I understand why."

"Okay. The police have his name and will do all the follow-ups necessary, so let's leave him to them," he said. "Who do you work with on a daily basis?"

"Martin, of course, and Jane, too, but the person after me is a man."

"Is Jane married?" he asked.

"She's a widow. Her husband served in the New Mexico Army National Guard and was killed last year by a roadside bomb," Holly said. "She's still in mourning."

"Let's talk more about Martin, then. He's physically fit, and about the same size and shape as the guy after you," Daniel said.

"No way he's behind this," Holly said. "Have you forgotten that he's the one who insisted I get protection?"

"That could be a smoke screen. I've seen him jogging and working out with our security people. Unlike most of those desk jockeys, he can hold his own."

She shook her head. "Martin's big and fit, but he's also a wuss. He almost passed out once when his new office assistant, Joe Yazzie, cut his finger."

"What about Joe? I haven't met him yet."

"He couldn't run that fast if his life depended on it. He's the size of a sumo wrestler with the strength to match. If he'd pinned me to the ground, that alone would have killed me."

"Then let's focus on Martin. The person who attacked you

on the street didn't try to stab you. He tried to strangle you—that's bloodless," Daniel said. "Martin also knows your routine and where you live."

"Okay," Holly said, giving up for now. "I have my doubts, but he'll stay on the list."

"Is there someone who might have a thing for you?" Daniel pressed.

"Thing?"

"The hots—romance, dating, sex."

"There's no one like that in my life. It's been months since my last date, and I don't dress the part or flirt. That tends to take care of things."

"Not so much. Maybe you're not aware of it, but men like looking at you."

Her heart jumped and she hid a pleased smile. Not looking directly at him, she tried to focus, though what she really wanted to do was ask if that included him.

She took a breath. "Besides Clyde Keeswood, there's another activist the plant's had some problems with, Johnny Wauneka. He's not the kind to shout out in a meeting, though. He's a highly intelligent, quiet computer nerd. Martin told me that he hacked into the plant's email accounts twice. They can't prove it, but they know it's him because he embarrassed the tribe in various blogs right after those incidents. I was also told that he made several suggestive remarks about me."

"Like what?"

"Nothing threatening, just remarks suggesting that I'm Martin's girlfriend and I'm scrambling his thinking—only written in a more graphic way."

"Have you responded to any of those posts?" Daniel asked.

She shook her head. "I don't want to legitimize them with a reply."

"That makes sense," he said. "Can I use your computer? I'd like to run Wauneka's and Keeswood's names through some databases. I'm also going to look up Jane Begay and Martin while I'm at it."

She stepped aside and waved him to her desk. Daniel sat down and accessed a website she'd never seen before. A box asking for a password popped up and she looked away. "Do you want me to step outside for a moment?"

"No need," he answered, typing away.

A new screen opened, and she saw Daniel enter Martin Roanhorse's name.

"I can't believe that you're actually checking on the man you work for," she said. "You *know* Martin."

"Nobody *really* knows anyone else," he said. "And for the record, I don't work for Martin, I just report to him. The tribe hired me and I'm looking after my client's interests."

"Interesting point of view," she said.

"You may not have noticed, but I've seen the way Martin checks you out when he thinks you're not watching."

"*Martin?* You've got to be kidding. His main interests are his wife, those quarter horses they raise and, of course, his ranch, just off the Rez. It's huge. He invited a handful of us to a party there last June."

"Big off-Rez acreage on a tribal bureaucrat's salary?" Daniel asked, quickly looking up.

"I know what you're thinking, but I was told that he got the money from his wife's parents. They're well-off," Holly said. "Martin likes his lifestyle and wouldn't do anything to jeopardize it."

He typed something else in, then nodded. "You're right. Martin's wife is a Markham. That family has ties to almost every major industry in the state. Bureaucrats can be vulnerable to corruption…." He let the sentence hang for several moments. "We can't discount anyone until we've got a solid reason to do so, like an unbreakable alibi."

"Okay. What about Johnny Wauneka?" she asked, looking at the monitor.

Daniel typed the name, then a new screen opened. "From what I see here, he has a few priors, but no felony convictions. The police never could get enough evidence to prove that he'd hacked into the tribal computer system."

"Wait—are you accessing a police database?" she asked.

"Yeah. I've got limited access. It's a courtesy," he said. "Detective Bowman arranged it for me."

She knew the value of connections, but this kind of trust was usually based on something more than loose friendship. Questions filled her mind and she found herself more curious than ever about Daniel.

"I recognize that look. What do you want to know?" he asked, smiling.

The fact that he'd read her so easily bothered her, but not enough to keep from taking advantage of what she saw as a golden opportunity. "Why does Bowman trust you so much?"

"It's earned. In every way that counts, Preston Bowman's my brother. He knows that I'd never betray him."

"Do you mean you're as close as brothers but not actually related?"

"We're part of a larger foster family."

"How many brothers and sisters do you have?" she asked.

"*Hosteen* Silver, our foster father, brought a total of six boys into his home. We came two at a time because we were hard cases, but he changed all our lives. What binds us now is stronger than blood ties—it's respect for the man who taught us about family and turned us into the men we are today."

"I have a feeling you've lived a very interesting life."

"Maybe so," he answered, shifting his attention to the computer once again.

"Tell me one more thing," she said, sensing he was reluctant to talk about himself. "If you had to describe yourself, what would you say?"

"Devastatingly handsome, sexy, available and incredibly good at his job."

"And humble."

He laughed. "Do you want someone who backpedals when asked if he thinks he's good, or someone who knows he is?"

"Okay, then let's skip to something I don't know," she said, laughing.

"In the Army I served with military intelligence. I was trained to gather and interpret information used to evaluate risks and protect targets," he said, then looked up and met her gaze. "You can trust me. While I'm on the job, nothing's going to happen to you."

There had been no hesitation in his voice. If nothing else, she knew he believed it.

"Yet you're still afraid," he observed.

She looked away, avoiding his steady gaze. "I just don't want to be completely dependent on your skills—or anyone else's—to survive. I need to shoulder at least some of that responsibility myself. Feeling helpless…it's no way to live."

"I hear you, but you also need to trust me. I *can* equalize the odds against you."

"The person after me is biding his time and studying our reactions. He's searching for something that'll give him a clear advantage. He wants to make sure that next time he strikes, he'll succeed," she said in a whisper. "I can't tell you how I know that, but I'm right. I feel it in my bones."

"Then we'll have to use those tactics against him."

"How?" Holly heard the fear in her voice and swallowed hard before continuing, "I'm a planner. I feel better when I look ahead and know what I need to do. That keeps me ready."

"Plans and tactics are good, but only if they don't hem you in and give you a bad case of tunnel vision. To stay safe you need to keep your options open," he said. "We'll need to stay flexible, move fast and change our plans on the fly. An unpredictable target is harder to hit."

"Okay, so what's next?" she asked.

"Let's go see Johnny Wauneka right now," Daniel said,

standing. "We'll take him by surprise and see what we can get out of him."

"People open up to me because I don't intimidate them. Let me handle this once we get there."

He smiled. "Works for me."

Chapter Eight

Daniel enjoyed the company of women. He liked the way they moved and the soft scents that clung to them, stirring his senses. They brought adventure and challenges into his life. Yet women invariably ended up wanting more than he was willing to give—of his time or himself—so he'd learned to avoid long-term relationships.

When Martin had first suggested that he provide security for Holly, he'd wanted to turn the job down. It wasn't part of his contract and he wasn't legally bound to accept. It was one thing to help Holly in a time of crisis, and another to actually stick around for the long haul. He wasn't a bodyguard—he was an analyst and instructor.

Yet something deeper had kept him from walking away. He admired Holly's courage, and that vulnerability she tried so hard to keep hidden tugged at him. He knew what it was like to feel targeted and alone. His days in foster care off the Rez, before coming to live with *Hosteen* Silver, were permanently etched in his memory.

Holly's streak of independence and the way she didn't give up, even when the odds were stacked against her, drew him to her. He knew nothing could ever come of it, but despite logic, when he looked at her, he found himself wondering what she'd be like if he kissed her. Would she fight him like a wildcat, or melt against him with a soft sigh?

"What are you thinking about?" she asked.

He clenched his jaw. He knew better than to allow himself to get distracted. "Did you know Clyde Keeswood has a brother?" he said, changing the subject. "His name is Nelson. It popped up when I was looking at your case file."

"I've never met him," she said.

"He has no priors, but there are other databases I can access that might tell us more about him," he said.

"I have no problems visualizing you as someone who spearheads war games and training exercises, but a techno-geek behind a computer? That's a tough one," she said with a smile.

He chuckled. "These days the most serious security breaches take place online via hackers. A thumb drive smuggled into a crucial facility can contain software and viruses that could do as much damage to an organization as a bomb. In a year or so, I plan to have people working for me who can deal with those threats while I stay out in the field. I'll be expanding my company and opening new offices in Phoenix and Denver."

"That'll mean you'll always be on the go," she said.

"Exactly," he said. "It'll be perfect, traveling, always facing new challenges." He smiled. "Will you eventually move on to bigger things, too?"

"Expansion isn't for me. I've finally found a place to call home and I'm happy here."

"You could call many places home," he said, watching her for a moment, then focusing back on his driving.

"To me, if it's really home, there's only one."

He kept his gaze on the road. So, despite the fact that she was a career woman with her own company, it appeared that inside Holly beat the heart of a nest builder. She was the kind of woman he normally avoided—the home-and-hearth type.

"Were you already living on the Rez when you were taken to *Hosteen* Silver's home?" she asked.

"No."

She waited patiently but when he didn't elaborate, continued, "Sorry. Sometimes I cross the line between curiosity and just plain nosiness," she said, then in a no-nonsense tone, added,

"Now that we're on the road, is there something you'd like me to stay on the lookout for besides an obvious tail? We need to stick to business."

Was that also a warning to him? If so, she was right. He wasn't the type of man she needed. Yet there was an innocence about Holly, an optimism about life, that urged him to protect her, particularly from himself.

He clenched his jaw. Though she was sitting close enough for him to touch, in the ways that mattered she was destined to stay out of his reach forever.

"Earth calling," Holly said after a long silence.

"I heard your question," he answered.

"Then it must be the way you listen. You don't move a muscle. It's as if you were miles away."

"Nope, I'm right here, but I'm also monitoring everything around us," he said. "Stillness is part of active listening."

She glanced behind them. "No one's following us, right?"

"No. I don't miss much, but it would help if you'd keep an eye on vehicles parked beside the road. If you see anyone pulling out as we pass, or just standing there watching passing cars, let me know."

He saw her squirm, worried. "It's just a precaution," he said.

They soon entered a run-down residential neighborhood. "I'm glad it's broad daylight. This is one off-campus area I wouldn't want to visit after dark," she said.

"You're safe."

"You're trying to make me feel better and I appreciate that, but I'm smart enough to know that we can always meet someone who's bigger than you or better armed."

"Even so, I can meet trouble and stay on my feet." He met her gaze for a second. "I'll make sure you walk away untouched."

Her eyes grew wide and she gave him a shaky smile. "I don't want you to get hurt, either."

"The other guy has more to worry about. I'm well trained

and at the top of my game. If I had any doubts about that, I wouldn't have agreed to help you find answers."

"I believe you," she said after a beat.

"Tell me more about your business, your company," he said, keeping his voice casual. If he was going to protect Holly, he needed to know more about her.

"I *never* accept jobs that go counter to what I believe in," she said. "I also refuse to work as a blame retardant—covering up a wrong by drowning it in fancy words and justifications. If a company wants to misdirect the public, they need to hire someone else."

"What if you take a job, then find out things aren't as above-board as you thought?"

"Then I do what I think is right, even if it means returning my fee and canceling my contract."

He nodded, liking what he heard. It confirmed his overall impression of Holly. After Martin had asked him to let her sit in on their latest security training exercise, he'd done a background check on Ms. Gates. Although he'd found nothing unusual about her, there'd been volumes on her father. A professional gambler, he'd lived life half a step ahead of trouble.

Daniel had met men like Clayton Gates before. They were always looking for that one big score at the tables. Yet even when they had a run of good luck, they'd lose it all by going back for more. They were addicted to the thrill of gambling, and it trapped them and their families in an endless cycle of empty promises and broken dreams. It was a roller-coaster ride that always ended up at the bottom.

"We're here," Daniel said at last, parking in front of a small apartment complex. To the right of that was what looked like an abandoned house.

"Which apartment is his? I don't see any mailboxes."

"Actually, Wauneka lives in the house," he answered. "I don't like to park directly in front of a suspect's home."

"To avoid placing yourself in the line of fire?" she asked.

He nodded, liking the way she could put things together. That might come in handy somewhere along the way. "They also tend not to see you coming, so the subject has less time to escape out the back door."

"Remember that we're trying to avoid putting him on the defensive. Think persuasion, not confrontation," she said.

"No problem," he said. "If I sense trouble of any kind, I'll tell you it's time to go. Don't argue, then, just do it."

"What kind of trouble could there be—?"

"Keep in mind that this could be the home of the man who tried to kill you and failed. If so, he might try again. Once we go in, we play it by my rules."

"Okay," she said.

They went to the front entrance and knocked. A moment later a Navajo boy in his late teens came to the door. Though it was cold, he was wearing a short-sleeved sweatshirt and a loose pair of jeans.

"I know you," he said looking at Holly. "And you're what, tribal Secret Service?" he added, looking at Daniel. "Guys, if someone hacked into the tribal network again, it wasn't me. You're wasting your time."

She smiled and shook her head. "I'm Holly, and that's not why we're here, John. Or do your friends call you Johnny?"

"John will do. What's up?"

"We just want to talk, John."

"Really? Why do I have a problem believing that?"

"Could we come in? It's kinda cold out here," Holly said, folding her arms in front of her.

"Yeah, okay," Johnny said, backing inside and letting them enter. "But the only reason I'm letting you inside my private residence is because, unlike you two, I've got nothing to hide."

Except for the sheepskin rug reminiscent of what you'd find inside a hogan, the living room looked more like a cheap storefront office than a residence, complete with a glowing electric space heater against a bare wall. There were three wooden folding chairs and a large dinner table that doubled as a desk. It stood against the wall on the opposite side of the room and was covered with stacks of manila folders and a take-out pizza box. A desktop computer was placed in its center, and beside it, an ink-jet printer and an open bag of potato chips. Next to the keyboard was a mouse and a tall can of one of those high caffeine energy drinks.

Johnny sat on the sheepskin rug and gestured for them to do the same. As Holly started to sit down, he gave her a slow, calculating smile. "I hope you like rats. Steve's AWOL right now."

She met his gaze, trying to figure out if he was purposely trying to freak her out. Refusing to react, she smiled back pleasantly. "I've had pet rats before, mostly classroom refugees. One was Hooded, a white and brown variety, and the other a big Dumbo. They're called that because of the size of their ears. Those are really cute. Tell me more about Steve."

He seemed surprised, but after a beat, answered, "He's large and white, just a big lab rat. He was going to be euthanized, so I adopted him."

Holly could see that he was disappointed in her reaction. He'd probably hoped that just the thought of a rat would send her running. "Do you know what I do for the tribe?"

"Yeah, spit out sound bites to mislead the public and keep the investors happy. How else can you suck them in?"

"Sounds like you're the one adding the spin. Smart decisions require objectivity. Have *you* bothered to search out and study the facts?"

"Facts, or fiction? I've read the materials you've released, but as the *Diné* say, everything has two sides. I want to know the other part—what you're not mentioning. The spin you put on the process makes it sound great, but people like me won't be satisfied with just PR feel-good statements. We'll keep looking until we find the whole truth."

"Everything I've presented *is* accurate," Holly said, keeping her voice soft and nonconfrontational. "You're looking for problems where none exist." Holly got up, walked quickly to his computer and reached behind it.

"Hey! Hands off! What do you think you're doing?" He jumped up, but before he could rush to where Holly was, Daniel blocked him.

Holly turned around a second later holding a large, white, domestic rat in her hands. "Steve, I presume?"

Johnny relaxed, and Daniel stepped back, allowing Wauneka to take the rat.

"He might have chewed through your cords," Holly said.

"Yeah, he does that from time to time. I've wiped them with chile sauce to discourage him, but I think he likes it hot. I better put him back in his cage."

As Wauneka carried the rat down the hall, Holly followed. On the way they passed a small bedroom that also doubled as an office. A second computer was on a desk, and a large cork board and a dry-erase board were mounted on the back wall.

Holly, hearing Wauneka putting Steve in his cage, stepped into the second office and read what was written on the dry-erase board.

"What the—" Daniel said, standing directly behind her.

"Hey, you guys have no right to go in there," Johnny said a moment later from the doorway.

Holly stood her ground, staring at the names. One of them was hers. The others belonged to people associated with the plant—everyone from energy companies, private investors, to Martin Roanhorse and the tribal president.

"What's this all about?" she demanded, pointing.

"It's exactly what you see—a list of the tribe's enemies," he said. "Didn't the word *Enemies* at the top give it away just a little bit?"

"You decided to include the tribal president?" she asked.

"He's the one pushing the new natural gas extraction process."

Catching a glimpse of a strange mobile in the corner of the room by the window, Holly stepped over for a closer look. Little corn-husk dolls were hung by their necks with cords tied in miniature hangman's nooses. They each had initials printed on them. One held her own, H.G.

"What's that—some kind of vision of the future for those you consider your enemies?" Daniel said before she could find her voice.

"Is it just wishful thinking, or part of a hit list?" she managed after a pause.

Wauneka shrugged and gave them a mirthless smile. "Naw, just motivation for the cause. It's also my way of amusing myself."

"Was attacking Holly last night your version of entertainment, too?" Daniel demanded, staring into his eyes.

Johnny's expression changed to one of total confusion. "Attacking who, her?" he asked, then quickly added, "Man, are you nuts? What the hell are you talking about?"

"Don't play dumb," Daniel growled, taking a step closer.

"Someone tried to strangle me," Holly said in a softer voice, pointing to the bruises on her neck. "Don't you watch the news? Or did you already know?"

As if a door had slammed shut, Johnny's expression went from alarm to closed, and impossible to read. He turned away and stepped out into the hall. "That's it. Time for you two to leave," he said, gesturing toward the living room.

"Are you saying that you're guilty, and you'd rather not comment without an attorney present?" Daniel pressed, following him into the hall.

"Leave." Johnny went to grab Holly's arm, but Daniel cut him off, forcing his back against the wall. "Careful," he growled. "Don't touch the lady."

"I want you two out of here—*now*." Johnny gestured toward the front of the house. "Move."

"If you're guilty, John, save yourself some time and a lot of grief. Come clean now," she said in the same soft tone.

He sidestepped her, his hands up near his shoulders for Daniel's sake. Once he was back in the living room, he stopped by the front door and spun around to face them. "When I fight, words are my only weapon. You can believe that or not—your choice—but you're going to have one heck of a time proving I'm guilty of anything. Last night I attended a very public forum at the community center for everyone who has concerns about the project. A lot of people saw me there, including Clyde Keeswood."

"In other words, people who'd alibi you anyway," Daniel shot back.

"Maybe, but the fact remains that you can't prove I was someplace I wasn't." Johnny opened the door, then waited only until they stepped out onto the porch before slamming it shut.

Holly glanced at Daniel as they walked to his SUV. "So much for a pleasant chat."

"It was worth the trip. We uncovered some interesting facts."

"Despite what we saw in there," Holly said, getting into the passenger's seat, "I don't think he's responsible. He strikes me as a loner, but not a killer," she said as they drove away from Johnny's place.

"Why, just because he rescued a rodent?" Daniel made a face. "That thing was big enough to eat a cat."

"It's harmless. They're raised for docility. That's why they can be handled in laboratory situations."

"I guess I'm used to the alley-trash-can-feral kind—complete with big teeth and the plague."

"That's a different creature altogether," she said. "Wild animals tend to act and react accordingly," she said. "All things considered, I think Johnny's just a lonely man who's trying to find a sense of purpose."

"I can't tell you how many times I've heard predators and

killers described, even by their next-door neighbors, as really nice people who seemed perfectly harmless."

"Maybe so, but in this case, I think what we're seeing is a man whose intellect and personality alienate him. All he's really got are his computers, a pet rat and the hope that he's doing something to protect the tribe. His home was…soulless."

"That's precisely what makes him dangerous," Daniel said.

Chapter Nine

As they reached the highway, Holly shifted in her seat and faced Daniel. "Why don't we go see Nelson Keeswood next? Clyde isn't going to give us anything useful, but maybe his brother will be more cooperative."

Daniel pulled over to the side of the road and stopped. Using his smart phone, he accessed a couple of databases. "Nelson lives with his brother, Clyde. I recognize the address. Clyde works at Car Magic in Shiprock, so he's not likely to be there now, but Nelson's a bartender at the Desert Oasis in Hartley. He works nights and might be at home."

It took them twenty-five minutes to reach a rectangular-shaped housing development several miles south of Shiprock, off Highway 491. Daniel drove up to the last house in the southwestern corner of the development. In the distance to the east was the southernmost tip of Hogback, protruding from the desert like the rock-hard spine of a sand dragon. To the south lay more barren, dry desert, punctuated by tabletop mesas.

"This looks to be a new Modernist area," Daniel said, after studying the isolated development.

"Good, then we won't have to sit in the car and wait to be invited in," she said.

As they got out of Daniel's vehicle, a short, thin, young Navajo man came out of the house and stood by the front door, waiting.

"I heard you drive up," he said when Daniel and Holly

reached the front porch. "Now that I see you up close, I recognize you, too."

"Have we met before?" Holly asked him.

"No, but my brother and I are familiar with everyone who's associated with the natural gas plant and the new projects."

"That's one of the reasons we're here. I wanted a chance to talk to you away from the crowds where you don't have to play a particular position. Ask me whatever you want. I'll do my best to give you an honest answer."

"What are the other reasons you came?" he asked. "This isn't a PR visit."

"I'm hoping we can help each other out," Holly said honestly.

"Why would I want to help you?" he countered.

"After all the mistakes that have been made in the past, I can understand why your group is suspicious of new industries, but resorting to violence isn't the answer."

He considered it for a moment. "All right. Come in and let's talk."

"Thank you," she said, and went inside the small foyer, Daniel half a step behind her.

As soon as Daniel stepped into the house, Nelson blocked his way. "You're the security expert the plant hired. Why are *you* here?"

"To watch, listen and understand," Daniel said.

Holly could see that Nelson wasn't satisfied with Daniel's answer. "You mentioned security. Well, frankly I asked Mr. Hawk to come with me because I've never been to this neighborhood, which is out in the middle of nowhere. Threats have been made against me, you may have heard the news, so I didn't want to come alone."

Nelson nodded, then led them into the adjoining living room and sat down. A half-dozen hand-painted protest signs attached to wood lath handles were stacked against the wall. "I get my share of threats, too."

She hadn't expected this. "What do you mean?"

"New gas exploration will mean jobs. Some say it's better to have money for groceries today than it is to worry about some undefined future. What people don't understand is that it all catches up to you."

While she was concentrating on Nelson, Daniel moved to a window and stood there, looking outside. Daniel's apparent lack of interest seemed to help Nelson relax.

"Have the threats against you been strictly verbal?" Holly asked, wondering if Daniel had purposely walked away, or whether he was searching for something or someone outside.

"Yeah, just words, so far, anyway," Nelson said. "The problem is that many of our people live day to day, barely getting by. The Rez has fifty-six percent unemployment and forty-three percent of us live below the poverty line."

"Then doesn't the immediate need—that of jobs—supersede a danger that might never materialize?"

"Some would agree with you," he said with a shrug. "We don't."

"Your group opposes new exploration, I get that, but does that also make you the enemy of anyone working to make it happen?" Holly asked, giving her words no particular emphasis.

Nelson leaned back. "I know where you're headed with that. You were physically attacked and you're looking for someone to blame, but if you think my group was responsible, you're way off base. Those kind of tactics would end up labeling us as extremists." He leaned forward, resting his forearms on his thighs. "To win this fight, we have to sway public opinion, and we can't do that if we're seen as criminals—or fools."

She considered his words as she tried to make up her mind about Nelson. His whole demeanor was one of a person struggling to get ideas across, not a dangerous vigilante ready to spill blood for his cause.

"Helping us identify the person who's coming after me would help prove that you're law-abiding citizens, and want no part of something like that. Would you be willing to let us know if you hear anything?" she asked, glancing at Daniel, who still hadn't said a word, then back at Nelson.

"Of course. That's in both our interests," Nelson said without hesitation.

Holly stood. "Thanks, and when you have some time, give me a call," she handed him her business card. "You and I can sit down and talk at length about the new extraction process. I'll take you through it step by step and answer all your questions. It *is* safe."

"I may take you up on that," he said. "We're not unrealistic. We just want to make sure jobs don't come at the expense of everything else."

"If I thought that could happen, I wouldn't have taken the job as spokesperson," she said.

"I think you mean that," Nelson said after a moment.

"Every word," she answered.

Once they were back in Daniel's car, Holly glanced over at him. "You were so quiet in there. How come?"

"You had it handled, and I was busy gathering other kinds of information. Regardless of how logical, levelheaded and plausible what he said seemed to be, there are things that don't add up."

"Like what?" she asked.

"According to the quick background check I did on them, even with donations, Clyde and Nelson barely make enough to keep body and soul together. Yet the pickup I saw parked in the back was brand-new and has a lot of optional extras."

"Maybe it doesn't belong to either of them."

"I checked, and the plates match. The pickup belongs to Nelson."

She stared at him, thinking about what he'd just told her. Daniel had been so quiet that somewhere along the way she'd concluded that he'd decided to stand back and remain a silent watchman. Instead, he'd been just as busy as she'd been.

"What else did you find out?" she asked.

"His boots."

"What about them?"

"He had a pair of hiking boots in the corner of the room—brand-new—but one of the boots had no shoelaces."

It took her a beat to take in what he meant. She swallowed hard. "Do you think the man who tried to strangle me used a shoelace to do it?"

"You were bruised not cut. You also told the police it wasn't wire, more like corded cloth, remember?"

Holly nodded. "Yet what Nelson said was true—violent acts would destroy his credibility, as well as that of his group."

"Violence also focuses attention on the issues and could benefit them in the long run. They can feed on the emotional publicity those incidents generate, just as long as there's nothing that can link back to them. The article in the newspaper is a prime example of that."

"I didn't see it. What did the article say?" she asked.

"They identified you and the work you do for the tribe. Although they didn't say that the attack was connected to your current assignment, they did say that the police were looking into all the possibilities."

"So the association was made by inference, which still results in bad press for the tribe." She expelled her breath in a soft hiss and shook her head. "I hear what you're saying and you've made some good points, but that's still not the *feel* I got from Nelson," she said.

"Suppose he's a better liar than you give him credit for?"

"Then we're going to need more than a missing shoelace and a shiny pickup to show the police, aren't we?" Holly said.

"Nelson needs to stay on our radar, at least for now."

Daniel had almost reached the highway when a pickup with three men in the cab raced toward them.

Holly stiffened, bracing herself for a collision.

Daniel cursed, swerving hard to the right, and the pickup

hurtled past them. The SUV swayed and kicked up a cloud of dust, but held traction. "What the—"

Holly turned around in her seat and looked back. "You think they're going to Nelson's?"

"They looked angry, and my bet is they're looking for trouble. Hang on. I'm heading back there." Daniel hit the brakes, skidded in the gravel, then whipped the vehicle around, sliding to rest in the opposite direction.

"Wait, what are you planning to do? There were *three* men in the cab. They could be armed," she said, reaching for her cell phone. "Let me call for help. You're going to be outnumbered." She tried several times to dial, but there was no signal. "No bars."

"Try mine," he said, pointing to the one resting on the console between them.

"Nothing," she said after a moment, "but maybe when we reach the top of this rise we'll have some luck. The problem is that there aren't too many cell towers between here and Gallup."

"The entire Four Corners is plagued with dead zones," he replied. "Someday, I'm getting a satellite phone."

She was still waiting for a connection when they drove up to Nelson's house. The pickup that had nearly sideswiped them was parked out front, but there was no sign of trouble.

"Everything's quiet. Maybe we misjudged the situation." Just then Holly heard angry shouts.

The front door suddenly burst open and two barrel-chested Navajo men came out, dragging Nelson by the arms. Though he was struggling, it was clear that Nelson had already lost the fight.

Then a third man, obviously working with the pair who'd overpowered Nelson, stepped into view. The man was massive, like a brick wall with legs. He was almost as wide as the doorway and looked as if he bench-pressed horses.

"Stay in the SUV and lock the doors," Daniel ordered, then

climbed out without looking back. "Hey, boys. Need some help with the little guy?" he called out.

"Move on, *hosteen,*" the short, hefty guy snapped, "or you're next."

Nelson looked at Daniel, winked, then went completely limp. The man on Nelson's left side suddenly lost his grip and Nelson fell to the ground, yanking his other arm free on the way down.

Nelson scrambled to his feet just as Daniel shot forward.

"Get him," the stubby guy said, rushing Daniel, head and shoulders down and arms out like a defensive tackle.

Daniel held back a beat, timing it just right. At the last second he dodged left, throwing out his right leg and tripping the onrushing bull of a man. The guy grunted and fell on his face onto the gravel.

"Help!" Nelson punched blindly at the men trying to renew their hold on him. He caught one in the chest, but it didn't even slow the man down.

Ignoring the man he'd just tripped, Daniel moved toward the one closest to Nelson. The guy swiveled on the balls of his feet, throwing a roundhouse left at Daniel's face.

Daniel ducked, throwing a right uppercut at the man's extended arm, catching him in the crux of his elbow. The man yelled in pain and sagged back. The third man grabbed Daniel's left wrist, twisting it at the same time he tried to shake off Nelson, who'd jumped on his back, his arm wrapped around the man's massive neck.

Nelson's weight threw him off balance and he let go of Daniel's arm just as Daniel slammed the heel of his right hand into the center of his chest. The guy fell like a tipped-over refrigerator, pinning Nelson beneath him.

Hearing the onrush, Daniel kicked back, aiming for the face of the short guy who came at him. The guy ducked under the kick, picking up Daniel's leg and heaving him to the ground.

Three men were on the ground now, twisting, punching and kicking to get free.

As Daniel rose to a crouch, Nelson behind him, he found himself staring down a wall of muscle. If the trio all rushed him now, he'd go down no matter what.

Suddenly an earsplitting whistle broke his focus. "That's enough!" Holly snapped, removing her fingers from her mouth. She waved her cell phone. "I've called the police, boys, and a cruiser with two officers is making the turn off the highway right about now. I've also got plenty of photos. Unless you want to spend Christmas and the New Year in a jail cell, I'd take the road out of here right now!"

The three muscle-bound guys exchanged glances, then raced to their pickup. Ten seconds later, they sped away in a cloud of dust and gravel.

Holly stepped over to Daniel and was glad to see he'd come out of the fight without a mark. Then she looked at Nelson. His eye was starting to swell and he had the beginnings of a nasty bruise on his cheek, but the only blood came from a cut on his lip.

"You'll both be okay," she said, breathing a sigh of relief.

"That was fast thinking," Nelson said, dabbing his cut lip with the back of his hand. "But how did you manage to get a cell phone signal out here?"

"What signal?" she said with a smile. "And as far as those photos go, you were all going at it so fast I doubt if anything was in focus." She checked and laughed at the display. "Forget it. Everything except for the house is a blur."

"So it was all a *bluff*?" Nelson said, then laughed.

"Remind me never to play poker with you," Daniel said.

"You'd lose your shirt, buddy," she said with a hint of a smile as she took Nelson's arm and led him back inside to clean up.

Chapter Ten

They were on their way back to Hartley fifteen minutes later. "I wish Nelson had been willing to press charges," Holly said. "Just because they disagree with his politics, no one has the right to barge in and attack someone in their own home."

"The location really doesn't make that much of a difference, does it?"

"Yeah, I think it does. Home…that should be a sanctuary for a person, a place beyond the world's reach. I realize that's idealistic, but it's the way I feel."

He didn't answer.

"You disagree?" she asked after a long silence.

"If someone came after me, the location wouldn't make much difference. Fighting—and winning—would."

"I suppose it's a matter of perspective," she said.

"So where to next? Shall I take you home?" Daniel asked.

She checked her watch. It was five-thirty and close to dark now. "I'd appreciate it if you would drop me off there."

Less than an hour later, Daniel pulled up in Holly's driveway. Holly went to her mailbox, collected everything it held, then gave Daniel a smile. "Thanks for the ride. I'll be fine now."

"Before you go inside, let me check the interior and the backyard."

"There's no need. This a very quiet neighborhood."

"It wasn't the other night," Daniel said, glancing down the

block toward the coffee shop. "You've got to remember to stay on your guard until the guy who came after you is in jail."

"You're right," she said, unlocking the door, then stepping aside. The porch light was on, the switch triggered by a photo sensor. "Go on in. I'll wait here."

"I'll only need a few minutes, then I'll be on my way," he said, turning the knob.

When he switched on the inside light, the first thing that struck him was that the living room looked as if it had been beamed in from the past. The oversize furniture was, by and large, made of polished hardwoods, and the floor lamps all held stained-glass shades.

As he moved closer to the hall, he went past two wall mounted shelves that held an array of brightly, hand-painted rocks decorated to resemble ladybugs. They caught his eye and he smiled, but didn't linger.

After searching the house and spending a couple of minutes looking out back, Daniel returned to the living room where Holly now stood. "Okay, it's clear. You're safe."

"Thanks," she said, walking him to the door.

"Your place has personality. I particularly like that collection of painted rocks."

She shook her head and smiled. "When I was growing up there were times when my dad and I would need to raise cash in a hurry. To help, I made rock creatures and sold them. Ladybugs were my favorites, though I made fish, and even camels," she said, then looked away as if uncomfortable.

He took the hint and didn't pursue it. "Remember to keep the doors locked, the drapes drawn and stay away from the windows. A few precautions like that can go a long way," he said, focusing on security details.

"I'll be careful. Thanks again," she said, then after a second's hesitation added, "Before you go, would you like to have something to drink, maybe to help you stay awake on your drive home? I have flavored teas and coffees, too."

"Coffee would be nice."

"Which flavor would you like? I have English toffee, chocolate macadamia nut and cinnamon."

"Surprise me," he said.

To effectively protect Holly, he needed to get to know her habits and routines. This was as good an opening as he was going to get.

"Make yourself comfortable while I get things together," Holly said, going into the kitchen.

As he stood by the fireplace mantel, he studied a half-dozen photos of Holly with her father. One showed her at seven or eight with both parents.

Minutes later, Holly came out holding a circular tray. On it were two mugs, one decorated with colorful Christmas ornaments and the other striped like a candy cane with a bright red handle.

"The peppermint stick mug has chocolate macadamia nut coffee. The other is cinnamon coffee. Choose whichever one you think you'd like most."

Guessing that she'd probably prefer the chocolate, he chose the cinnamon coffee and took a sip. "It's good."

She laughed. "Don't act so surprised."

He smiled. "I'm more used to rot-your-gut black coffee."

She took a seat on the couch, slipped off her shoes and tucked her legs under her. "This is usually my favorite time of year. I was planning to get my Christmas tree this week. I love decorating it, then decking out the entire house. I usually put lights on all the windows and on some of the trees outside. What about you?"

"Not so much. When Gene and I lived with *Hosteen* Silver we followed Navajo traditions and Christmas wasn't something we went all out on. In fact, when we first came to live with him, the only holiday we celebrated was Thanksgiving. Eventually Gene and I, who were raised with Christmas, talked him into letting us put up a tree. We'd all go out, choose a piñon tree that seemed right, chop it down and bring it home. After the holiday was over, we'd dry it out and use the wood in the stove or fireplace." He glanced back at the mantel. "I noticed all the photos. Were you and your family close?"

She considered it before answering, and that pause told him far more than words alone could have.

"My mother passed away when I was seven. My dad…was hard to describe."

"Was? He's also gone?"

She nodded. "He died doing what he loved best—gambling. He was in Vegas at a poker tournament and slumped over dead at the table from a heart attack."

"He taught you to play cards? I remember you said that if we ever played poker, I'd lose," he said.

She smiled. "Yeah. I learned from the best, but I won't play, not even a friendly game. I've seen the dark side of gambling."

"The Navajo way teaches that everything in life has two sides. To walk in beauty, you need to keep all the elements of your life in their proper balance."

"Yeah, and when people can't do that, sometimes things fall apart." As soon as she spoke, she shook her head and looked away.

Daniel could see that she regretted telling him. "You're a private person, and I've intruded." He set the cup down and stood.

"Don't go yet. You didn't intrude. I volunteered the information," she said. "It's just that I'm uncomfortable talking about certain parts of my past."

"In that, we're alike," he said, taking his seat again. "So let's talk about something else. Tell me about this place. I know your home is special to you."

She smiled. "The house dates back to the early forties and it was a complete wreck when I bought it. Fixing up the outside was easy, but turning the interior into a real home was a lot harder, and it wasn't just the lath and plaster walls. To me, the perfect home has to have that same special warmth you get looking at Norman Rockwell paintings. Since we were always on the move when I was growing up, what I've tried to create here is a place that, like those images, speaks of permanence. Best of all, once I pay off the mortgage, this place will be all mine."

He considered what she hadn't said, and wondered how long she'd stared at the paintings she'd mentioned, ones he knew depicted so-called perfect American families and lifestyles. He looked around more slowly, taking everything in.

"Restoration means a great deal to you, doesn't it?" he asked.

"To me, it's more than just the act of restoring," she said, considering her words. "I see what I do as making a place for the old among the new." She stared at the floor, lost in the thought. "In my work, I sometimes see new technologies trampling over what has always been there, like nature. Yet both can coexist. It just takes effort, and the extra work pays off in the long run."

"Your way of looking at things isn't far off *Diné* teachings. We believe that all of life is connected. The way to harmony is to recognize the natural order of things and find your place within that."

"The *Diné* have beautiful traditions and beliefs. Like them, I try to walk in beauty."

He gazed at her, then fighting the attraction between them, looked away. "You're a woman of…layers," he said at last.

She took a cautious sip of her coffee. "You're making me sound like a rock formation. Was that a compliment?" she said, and smiled.

"You're like a beautiful image that shifts continually on a computer screen," he said, nodding. "Before you get a handle on what you're seeing, a new picture emerges."

"The same could be said of you. I've seen the warrior—the security consultant who's always on his guard, meeting trouble head-on. Yet your mentor was a *hataalii,* a man of healing and peace. I suspect there's some of that gentleness inside you, as well."

"Gentleness doesn't play well in my world."

As the grandfather clock began to chime, Holly glanced at the time. "It's getting late and I have to work for the tribe at the Winter Job Fair tomorrow," she said.

"The one at the Hartley Community Center? Bad idea," he said. "You're too exposed there."

"I'll take all the precautions you recommend, but if I let this man push me into hiding, I may never find my courage again. Then he really will have defeated me, whether or not he succeeds in killing me," she said. "You don't strike me as a person who has ever really known fear, Daniel, so I'm not sure you can understand my feelings about this."

"I do know fear. I just have my own way of dealing with it, that's all," he said. He thought back to his days as a kid on the city streets. Being the only Navajo around at times often singled him out to the bullies, and the gangs. Then he'd met Gene. They'd banded together to avoid getting jumped, finding new strength by becoming allies. "I focus solely on the threat and how to defeat it."

"What does it take to scare you, Daniel?" she asked. "I know that it's not being outnumbered or having to fight."

"No, neither of those." He remembered the night his mother hadn't come home. He'd just turned twelve. Days had gone by and eventually a neighbor had turned him over to foster care. He'd found out afterward that there'd been a fight at the bar where his mother had worked as a waitress. A stray bullet had ended her life. No one had ever come to claim him. Since he'd never known his father, he'd suddenly found himself all alone. He'd known terror then. "I fear what I can't fight," he said at last.

He saw the questions in her eyes, but instead of answering,

he stood. She rose, as well, and for a moment they were so close he could feel the warmth of her body.

"The guy you're up against is flesh and blood and can be defeated," Daniel said. "This is a battle we can win."

He brushed her face with the palm of his hand and saw her lips part slightly. Instinctively he leaned down and took her mouth in a slow, gentle kiss. She tasted the way she looked, delicate and sweet.

Her mouth flowered open, inviting him to take more, and a blast of heat slammed into him. He'd never passed up an invitation like this, but he had no choice but to walk away now, while he still could. Everything he knew about Holly assured him that she wasn't the kind to have an easy, friends-with-benefits type of relationship.

"I'll protect you, Holly, even from me," he growled, moving away from her and toward the door. "You don't owe me anything, not even a kiss. You're hard to resist, so I won't be turning any of those down, but you know what they say about playing with fire…." His voice rumbled like an approaching winter storm.

"A man of tenderness wrapped in danger…that's what *I* see."

He'd been called many things throughout his life, but no one had ever called him that. He wanted to kiss her again, but this time she was the one who moved away.

"Good night, Daniel," she whispered.

He opened the door, then turned his head before he stepped outside. "I'll pick you up tomorrow. What time?"

"Seven. Can you get here by then, or is that too early?"

"I think I'll manage somehow," he said, and smiled.

Soon he pulled out of her driveway. Unable to resist, he stopped in the street and looked back toward the house. The lights inside the small *casita* glimmered and danced just beyond the curtains. That soft glow called to him, whispering of secrets and longings that were not part of his world.

He shook free of those thoughts. He was tired and it was the holiday season, the time of year when old wounds ached, and outsiders were destined to remain just beyond the warmth.

Chapter Eleven

The Winter Job Fair was a semiannual event held in Hartley's new community center. Along with a few local government agencies looking for temporary workers, representatives from several of the major in-state industries came looking to fill a handful of open positions. The recession and the lack of jobs that plagued the economy all but guaranteed that they'd have a great turnout.

"You can pass as my assistant," she told Daniel as she set up the table.

"Fine, but I'd like to walk around first and get a feel for the people here. I won't be far."

"Okay," she said, her mind already on the brochures and application forms she was setting out on the table. Last night Martin's new assistant, Joe Yazzie, had placed the posters and assembled the booth for her. He'd done a great job, too.

As she glanced at the display in the booth next to hers, she tried not to cringe. Everything SunWest Futures did was legal, but she hated the way they recruited their students. What they promised their applicants and what the school actually delivered were two very different things.

She'd first heard about SunWest a year ago. They ran a highly profitable school that trained its students to assemble and install solar panels. They provided tuition loans and job placement services, but the company rarely delivered on the employment promises that were part of their sales pitch. What the students usually discovered, after spending a small fortune on tuition, was that the few local jobs in that field paid far less than promised, and most available positions were scattered all across the country. By then, they were also locked into high interest loans that bled them dry.

A few months ago, trying to find out if those stories were true, she'd agreed to meet with Ross Williams, one of their recruiters, for dinner. They'd both been at a job fair and she'd expected it to be nothing more than a quick mealtime break, but she'd been in for a big surprise. Ross, despite his respectable business suit and tie, turned out to be a real cockroach. He'd hit on her, refusing to take no for an answer and getting grabby. Out of options, she'd finally threatened to call the police.

Now here he was again, ripping people off with his smarmy sales pitch. Although she made it a point to avoid eye contact, he continued to look in her direction.

Knowing that Daniel was close by made it easier to work next to Ross and, before long, Holly forgot all about him. Many applicants had come to compete for the handful of jobs the tribe had to offer. As she answered questions and described the work locations and requirements, time slipped by.

After several hours of almost nonstop visitors, Holly was ready for a break. The crowd in front of her desk had moved on, though there were still several people filling out applications at SunWest.

As she glanced over, she saw Ross talking to two young Navajo men, one she recognized as the son of a gas company worker. More than anything, Holly wished she could have warned them, but there was nothing she could do. Frustrated, she decided to use the lull at her own table to grab a soft drink.

Walking around the fifteen-foot high Christmas tree in the center of the room, she headed to the wide hallway where the vending machines were located. It was off the main floor, and served as a passageway leading to the performing arts theater, which was empty today.

She looked at the drinks offered, and picked one without caffeine. She was amped up enough as it was.

"You next to me—it must be fate," a familiar, unwelcome voice said.

Holly turned around and saw Ross had followed her into the passage. "We have nothing to say to each other, Mr. Williams."

"Aw, come on. You still playing Miss Innocent? You're a player, I know it. I saw the look you gave me a minute ago."

"What you saw was disgust—for you and for your alleged job placement program. Those people believe you and you're ripping them off."

"Nah, they get great training. If they lack the ambition or resources to search out the best jobs, that's their problem. We just open the door, we can't take their hands and lead them through. Now what do you say we talk about us? I could have sworn you were offering me a second chance. Regrets from last time?"

"I regret that you're here and that you have the booth next to mine."

"I've got a feeling about you, Holly," he said quietly, coming closer. "Playing hard to get is foreplay for you, right? You're hot and you want a man who can get rough."

Suddenly afraid, she took a step back but ran into the wall. The last thing she wanted to do was make a scene here. The creep wasn't worth it, but he wasn't giving her many options. "Back off—now! I have to go back to work."

"Come on, baby. That's not what you really want and we both know it," he murmured in her ear, leaning forward.

He pinned her against the wall with a hand on either side, then began nuzzling her neck.

She kneed him hard in the groin. "I warned you," Holly said. *"Back off."*

He gasped, his eyes watering as he stepped back in a crouch. "You little tease—" He reached out his hand to slap her, but Daniel appeared out of nowhere.

He grabbed Ross's wrist, and applying some kind of nerve pinch, sent the man to his knees on the tile floor, groaning in agony.

Ross threw a punch with his other hand, but Daniel was out of reach and he simply increased the pressure. Ross squealed, his face contorted in agony.

"Settle down, or you'll embarrass yourself in front of three-hundred people," Daniel said in a cold-as-ice voice. "I can make this hurt a *lot* more."

"No, let go," Ross mumbled, looking toward the end of the passage. Three young people were watching them curiously.

"How about you and I go outside for a talk?" Daniel said. "I'll back off on the pain, let you stand and walk on your own power. Just don't screw with me or I'll take you down again."

"Okay, okay," Ross said.

Daniel motioned toward the far end of the tunnel. "Take the outside door on your left."

Holly started to follow, but Daniel turned and shook his head. "Stay here. Don't worry, I won't hurt him unless he insists."

Holly watched them go. Daniel was her protector, but as grateful as she was for his help, it also made her uneasy. Having a man like Daniel around, one who could keep trouble at bay, could be addicting. It was always easier to let go and allow someone else to handle the hard stuff—at least at first. Yet life had taught her that relying on another always came at a price.

As she thought of her dad her throat tightened. People invariably let you down if you counted on them. Disappointment followed and, in Daniel's case, maybe even heartbreak.

When the job fair finally came to an end at six and the doors were locked, Holly was more than eager to call it a day. She was exhausted. Hundreds of people had come to leave applications for the three-dozen job openings offered by the tribe. She'd seen the eagerness, and more often than not desperation in the eyes of the ones who'd come to her table. Jobs were too scarce these days and the inability to get employment often made people feel useless. That could trigger a long downward spiral that led only toward darkness.

She knew that road well. Her father had been a manager at a retail business for years. Then, faced with the store's sudden closing and mounting debts from casino losses, he began his lifelong search for that illusive big score. The more he'd gambled, the worse their lives had become.

Holly packed all her materials in boxes, and by the time she was ready to go, Daniel was back, after having excused himself to take one more look around the parking lot and display area.

"Williams left early, and hasn't returned. After we talked, I reported what happened to the police and event security. They'll both be speaking to him," Daniel said.

"In case you're wondering, I'm almost sure he's not the one who attacked me outside the café. Think about it—that's not what a cockroach does. A cockroach is a bottom-feeder, sneaky but predictable."

"You might be right," Daniel said with a shrug. "Either way, Preston will talk to him and let us know what he gets from him. In the meantime, you need to give more thought to other possible suspects. You never put Ross Williams on your list. Are you sure you haven't left anyone else out?"

"As I said, I don't consider Ross a suspect." She ran a hand through her hair. "The other people I deal with regularly are tribal employees, and you already know most of them. I'm sorry, but I just don't have the answers you want."

"All right. Where to now?" he asked.

"My office. I need to get these applications ready to mail to the tribal offices in Window Rock, and pick up some files," she said.

As Daniel drove, she glanced over at him. "I've just realized something. Your job's all about danger."

"No, not really. I'd say it's more about *anticipating* danger and making sure my tactics remain unpredictable to whatever enemy I'm fighting."

As she thought about what he'd said, she looked around, studying the route he'd chosen. They weren't heading to her office, or if they were, he'd chosen a long, roundabout way. Holly looked over at Daniel and immediately noticed the rigid set of his jaw and the way he kept glancing into the rearview mirror.

"What's going on?" she asked.

"We're being followed. What kind of car does Williams drive?"

"You think he's coming after us?" she asked, her voice rising.

"Answer my question. What kind of car does he drive?"

"A company car, at least the last time I saw him. It's a white, four-door sedan with a SunWest Futures sign on the doors."

"What make?" he insisted.

"I don't know, Ford, Chevy maybe. It's a sedan."

"This one's silver. Maybe he's got a new ride." Daniel used his Bluetooth. "Call Preston," he said, giving the command.

A moment later his brother answered. Daniel described the situation, listened, then hung up.

"They have an unmarked unit not too far from where we are. Once that vehicle's in position, we'll keep going while they box him in," Daniel said in a low growl.

"But that's not what *you* want to do," she said. As sure as she was of her next breath, she knew he wanted to confront the person behind them.

"If it were up to me, I'd force whoever's back there off the road, then…have a talk with him," he said at last. "But this is up to the police, and all things considered, the city's a poor location for a confrontation that might involve a high-speed chase. We'll just concentrate on ditching this guy once the cops are ready to take over."

Daniel made a sharp right, then cut to the left at the next

intersection. The silver sedan remained a half block away. After another three minutes, his cell phone rang.

"He's still with us," Daniel said after a beat. "No, no threatening moves, just tailing and maintaining his distance." He paused. "I could lead him into a trap. The warehouse district...."

Another pause.

"All right," Daniel answered at length. "I'll be passing the cruiser's location in another minute. As soon as the officer has eyes on the guy, I'll break off and head for my office while you handle things."

As Daniel turned the corner, he saw the unmarked police sedan, a make and model he recognized, parked by a fast-food place. Daniel drove past, nodding slightly for the officer's sake, then made a right turn and sped away. "It's up to the cops now."

Their tail followed them into the turn, then abruptly cut across traffic and disappeared up an alley behind a strip mall. The unmarked police car ended up being blocked by traffic and had to wait for the light.

"I wish they would have let me help, but Preston's in charge and he's a stickler for procedure. He'll choke on that rule book of his one day," Daniel said.

"Tell me about the others *Hosteen* Silver took in."

"We were all trouble, I mean Trouble with a capital T. That's the reason *Hosteen* Silver would only take on two kids at a time, though those of us who had already left were usually available to help, if needed. He turned our lives around. Without him, all six of us might have ended up in prison or dead on the street."

Daniel suddenly cursed.

"What's up?" Holly straightened up in her seat and glanced around.

"Our tail's still with us," Daniel said. "He must have doubled back and circled until he spotted us."

"Call Preston," she said instantly.

He shook his head. "We're out of his jurisdiction here in county. We're in a no-man's-land covered by a few deputies and the state police. It takes them forever to respond."

"Once we reach Hartley we can get Preston's help," Holly replied.

"We'll also give our tail a whole city to get lost in, *if* he follows us that far without turning back. No, I want to corner this guy, or at least get a good look before he knows we're on to him."

Holly nodded. "So do I. What do you have in mind?"

He glanced ahead at a cluster of businesses beside the highway. "Will you trust me? I've got an idea."

"Okay. How can I help?"

He smiled, thinking of how much he liked Holly. He slowed, then turned into the parking lot of the Bucking Bronco. "I'm hoping he'll follow us inside. If he does, he and I can...talk."

"This is a lousy place for that. If there's any problem, they'll put boxing gloves on both of you and throw you in a cage together to settle it."

"You've been here before?"

"No, but people talk."

"Don't worry. I'm a master of tact and diplomacy," he said, with a twinkle in his eye. "If that fails, and we end up fighting, I'll make sure he goes down, then hold him there for the cops."

"But what if something goes wrong?"

"I expect I'll take a few punches, but like you said, they make you wear heavy gloves. Those protect you somewhat."

"So *you've* been here before. I should have known," Holly said.

"Nah," he grinned. "Like you said, people talk."

They went inside and managed to find an empty table just as some oil workers were leaving. It was in the far corner, next to a square, ten-foot high enclosure made of chain-link fence and metal posts that extended from floor to ceiling.

To their right, extending from the far end of the bar, was a circular platform set around a shiny chrome steel pole. Narrow steps led up from the floor, and two spotlights illuminated the dancer's tiny stage.

"So they have a stripper, too?" Holly said as they sat down.

"How do you think all those fights get started?" Daniel said, then took a quick look around the room.

A tired-looking blond waitress wearing a tight T-shirt and baseball cap with a Bucking Bronco patch came over within a few seconds. "What can I get ya, honey?" she called over the din of country-western music coming from ceiling-high speakers. Her frozen smile and pale blue eyes were on Daniel.

"Draft. And how about you, babe?" Daniel answered, a wide grin on his face as he turned to Holly.

"A cola," she answered primly.

"Gotcha," the waitress replied, rolling her eyes at Daniel in mock sympathy. "Be right back."

Holly looked around at the patrons, mostly oil workers and a few cowboys judging from the blending of wide-brim hats, the scent of sweat and oil, and caps with company logos. "Now what? Did anyone follow us in?"

"Not yet, so we'll wait," Daniel said, checking the entrance again out of the corner of his eye.

Chapter Twelve

An eternity passed and a few regular customers came in, and were greeted by those inside the tavern. Yet no one paid any particular attention to them. Daniel had just left to talk to the bartender when a tall, muscular man with greased-back black hair and a day-old stubble stumbled in her direction. She tried not to make eye contact, hoping he'd veer away.

Unfortunately, seconds later, he placed a beefy hand on her shoulder. "They're playing our song, pretty lady. How about you get up and dance with me?"

"Um, no thanks," she said, turning away. The liquor on his breath was nearly overpowering.

"Come on, sweet thing. Just a spin or two around the floor." He reached for her hand, but just then Daniel appeared.

"She doesn't want to dance, friend," Daniel said. "Walk away."

"Out of my face, Chief," the man said.

As he reached for Holly's arm again, Daniel stiff-armed him in the chest, sending him reeling back three steps.

"You want a piece of me?" the man said, regaining his balance. "Come on, then. Let's do this."

A whistle suddenly split the air, so loud everyone turned to look. A big, barrel-chested man carrying a taped up baseball bat stepped out from behind the bar. He spit out the silver coach's whistle, then pointed the business end of the bat at Daniel, then to the burly thug.

"You two have a beef? You either take off with your tail

between your legs, or settle it like men. I'm talking *in the cage*—until somebody goes down or yells *uncle.* Whadda you say, you men, or crybabies?"

"This gentleman didn't mean any offense. He's just had too much to drink," Holly said quickly. "There's no need for a fight."

There were collective groans from all around the room.

"So what'll it be? You gonna hide behind the girl and run for the door?" the man said, getting into Daniel's face.

"Let me buy you a beer, and we'll call it even," Daniel said through clenched teeth.

"And here I thought you'd bleed red, not yellow."

Daniel shook his head, then looked at the bartender. "Get the gloves."

"You don't have to do this," Holly said, trying to reason with him. "We'll walk out."

Daniel leaned closer to her. "We'd never make it out the door without more trouble, trust me. This is a setup. Let me handle this guy first, then we'll go outside and look for the sedan."

All eyes were on Daniel and the big gorilla-looking guy who'd given his name as Roger as the cage door was opened, and closed behind them.

Roger immediately rushed Daniel, faking a punch to his face. Daniel slipped the punch, which brushed his cheek, and landed a solid blow to his attacker's chest. Roger's forward momentum carried him into Daniel, and they both crashed into the wire, then rebounded out.

The big man staggered back, launching a kick that caught Daniel in the thigh. Daniel grimaced in pain, then limped to the side, barely avoiding the solid connection from a roundhouse that glanced off his temple.

Everyone rose to their feet, shouting and placing bets.

Holly looked around, trying to figure out how to stop it. This had *not* been part of their plan. They were after the man who'd tailed them, not the hulk inside the cage.

"Put a stop to this," she yelled to the bouncer.

The man shook his head, and pointed to the floor, reminding her that this would end only when somebody went down.

As she moved toward the entrance, reaching for her cell phone, a figure came up from behind her. He grabbed her arm, and yanked her into the dark foyer. All she could see was a black baseball cap and that blue bandanna over his face.

"Let go!" As she struggled to break his hold, she realized that Daniel had been right. They'd been set up. Desperate, she rammed her elbow into his midsection and broke free.

Holly ran back inside, screaming, but the man followed her. Since everyone else in the Bucking Bronco was yelling, too, no one paid any attention to her. The crowd was focused on the pair fighting inside the cage.

A hand grabbed her shoulder and pulled her back hard toward the foyer again. Holly swung her fist around and connected with something, maybe the man's nose, and broke free.

She pushed her way through the rowdy crowd, most on their feet, but there was no place to run. Realizing that the man was closing in on her again, and out of options, she broke away from the screaming crowd, and ran for the stripper's platform. Grabbing the pole, she began doing an awkward dance.

Soon some of the men turned away from the fight to watch her. Roger, too, shifted his gaze, and that's when Daniel caught him with a right cross that sent him to the floor.

Holly knew she'd be safe as long as she remained the focus of the room. With that in mind, she unbuttoned the two top buttons of her blouse, then ducked down, showing some cleavage as the men cheered and whistled.

"Enough of this," Daniel said and slipped off the heavy boxing gloves. "Open the damned door," he yelled to the bouncer.

He stepped out, then pushed his way across the room and through the crowd clustered around the stripper's stage.

"Let's go, woman!" Daniel yelled, catching Holly's eye. He raised up his arms. "Jump."

She leaped off into his arms, wrapping her legs around him. He caught her, his eyes gleaming with an inner fire that any woman with a heartbeat would recognize.

Daniel whirled her around and kissed her as the men cheered. Though she'd expected something hard and possessive, his kiss was gentle, filled with tenderness despite the drama of the moment. Before she could catch her breath, he tossed her over his shoulder and walked toward the door. Everyone was still cheering, and as they reached the foyer the bouncer handed them their jackets.

"Ya'll come back, okay?" he said with a wide grin.

Once they were outside, Daniel set her down and they ran to the SUV.

"I lost the man following us, but you were right. It was a setup. Even with all those people around, he came after me in there," she said, telling him what had happened as they fastened their seat belts.

Daniel looked around the parking lot, but failed to see the sedan. "Maybe a BOLO will help," he said, and called Preston.

"My brother will be able to get the other departments involved now," he told Holly after hanging up.

"So now what? Where should we go?" she asked.

"*My* office. It's just outside Hartley, and it's impossible to get near that place without at least one set of cameras picking you up."

Twenty minutes later they arrived at a large rectangular warehouse enclosed by a tall chain-link fence on all four sides of the three-acre lot. Dried out alfalfa fields surrounded the grounds.

Daniel stopped at the gate, entered a code on a number pad, and the door slid open. As Daniel drove through, the gate closed behind them. Lights came on as they went closer to the building, which was located in the center of the property.

"I've refitted the place to fit the needs of my business. It used to be an old farm equipment warehouse that was repossessed by the bank," he said.

Once inside the metal, pitched roof building, Holly saw the place was mostly empty. There was a large desk in the center of the main room, and around that, freestanding dry erase and cork boards that held what appeared to be tactical maps. A rectangular glass table stood by itself just beyond the desk, but a power cable leading from the table to a wall outlet suggested it wasn't just a table.

Two desktop computers were against one side wall, along with several heavy, locked file cabinets. There were also bookshelves filled with what looked like technical journals and DVDs. Along the back, between two interior doors, was the kitchen area, complete with a refrigerator, small stove, several cabinets and a long counter. A round, bistro-style metal table with two chairs was nearby.

At the opposite end wall was a sitting area with a couch, two chairs and a coffee table, all enclosed within a low barrier comprised of stacked, painted cinder blocks.

"Make yourself comfortable," Daniel said, shrugging off his leather jacket. The plain dark blue wool sweater he wore over his collared shirt accentuated Daniel's broad shoulders and his lean middle.

"Are you sure you're okay?" she asked.

"Positive," he said. "I've taken worse in training ops." He gave her a heart-stopping smile. "I still can't believe what you did back at the Bucking Bronco. That was fast thinking. Until you got up on that platform everyone was watching the fight."

She shuddered, thinking about it and he pulled her into his arms.

Although she knew she should have moved away, his body felt hard, strong and oh, so good! "That little stage was the safest place for me to be."

"How far would you have gone?"

"Let's just say I was grateful you finished off Roger when you did," she said, stepping out of his arms.

His grin was slow and utterly masculine. "I didn't get to see much of that dance. Maybe you'll give me a repeat performance?"

His words teased her imagination. "In your dreams."

"I'll have plenty of those now," he said, his voice a rough whisper.

She shivered, then realizing that he'd seen her reaction, diverted his attention by pointing to the thermostat.

"Are you cold? I'll turn up the heat," he said with a nod, stepping over to the wall and pushing the up button on the programmable device. "I keep it at sixty whenever I'm not here."

"When do you usually get home?"

"Unless something's going on at night, I'm here by seven, give or take. Most of my work is done at the client's site, like at the plant. It's rare that I have to bring anyone here to my office because I prefer to train people on the turf they'll be protecting. When I bring personnel here it's to run computer simulations that'll showcase the potential risks to their facilities. They get an overview of the entire operation and can see exactly what needs to be done. I can demonstrate the results of an electronic or computer attack on their systems, too. That table over there is really a touch screen monitor that allows clients to view and evaluate potential threat scenarios in real time."

She thought of her own business office. Everything there, from the furnishings to the layout, reflected her personality. By contrast, Level One Security's office felt like command headquarters—all precision and focused objectives. Yet Daniel had a gentle side, too. Though he chose to keep it hidden, she'd felt its impact all through her when he'd kissed her.

"Are you hungry? I can make you something for dinner," Daniel said, interrupting her thoughts and gesturing toward the kitchen area.

Before she could answer, a tall, good-looking Navajo man wearing jeans, a loose blue corduroy shirt and boots entered the room from one of the two interior doors. "Don't let my brother fool you," the man said, flashing her a confident grin. "To him, a meal is two or three of those plastic dish meals that read 'peel back to vent.'"

"You here already?" Daniel said, trying and failing to suppress a grin. "This is my brother Gene. He's staying here for a while."

"In your office?" Holly asked, looking around again.

"Daniel lives here. There are two rooms in the back that hold cots and metal wardrobes—his version of bedrooms—so he calls it home," Gene said.

"As far as my brother's concerned, if there's no hay or tack visible and a couple of horses in the stalls, it can't possibly be a real home."

"Wait—you live *here?*" she asked Daniel, surprised.

Gene burst out laughing. "I bet that cut deep, bro." He gave her a big smile. "I'm Gene, the good-looking one in the family."

She didn't offer to shake hands, not sure if he was comfortable with the custom or not. "Pleasure," she said. "I'm Holly."

"Keep an eye on the monitors, will you?" Daniel said, updating his brother on recent events.

"No problem. You're safe here," Gene told Holly, then walked to one of the computers by the wall.

"Now, as I was saying before we were so rudely interrupted," Daniel said with a quick grin, "there are some cold cuts in the fridge that could make a great roast beef sandwich. You up for some food?"

"Just don't touch the sliced bread, Holly," Gene said. "It's got hairy gray stuff growing on it. Take some of the French bread I brought. It's sitting on the counter."

"Why didn't you throw out the moldy loaf?" Daniel asked, glowering at him.

"And spare you a bite of that penicillin? Hey, it's winter and you've got to keep your health."

"Freeloader. You're lucky I don't kick your sorry butt out of here," Daniel said, opening the refrigerator.

"Yeah, yeah. Strong words for a soft, city boy."

"You're welcome to put that to a test, farm boy," Daniel called back, then winked at Holly, who'd taken a seat at the round table.

From where she was sitting it was easy to see how different Gene and Daniel were from each other. Gene moved with slow measured strides. Daniel prowled along the counter like a tiger on the hunt, a symphony of confidence and focus. Just watching him made her fingertips tingle with the desire to touch him.

He met her watchful gaze and smiled. "I'm just a regular guy. No superpowers, no cape."

She smiled but said nothing, unsure of how to answer without revealing even more of what she'd been thinking. He could read her thoughts much too easily as it was.

Regardless of what he'd said, Daniel was far from ordinary. He had the courage it took to defy the odds and fight for what was right. Yet it was the magic she'd found in his arms that held her spellbound. It would be a long time before the memory of his last kiss faded from her mind.

"You and Gene are very different," she said, forcing her thoughts back onto safer channels.

He nodded, glancing at Gene, who was over by the monitors. "We were a lot to handle when *Hosteen* Silver first took us in. I'd turned fourteen and Gene was thirteen. I'd come from two years in foster care and Gene through four. *Hosteen* Silver never tried to preach to us, though. What he did was work our butts off hauling water, doing chores—*nothing* was taken for granted. By the end of each day we were beat, but we never had to worry about going hungry or staying warm in winter again."

"How come you didn't stay on the Rez?" she asked.

"*Hosteen* Silver taught us that to walk in beauty we'd need to find our own paths in life. For me, that meant serving in the Army, then starting my own business."

She nodded, still trying to figure Daniel out. The place he called home was Spartan at best. Even the kitchen was equipped only with essentials. The only things on the counter were the loaf of French bread Gene had brought, a small microwave and coffeemaker.

"We've got company," Gene called out.

Daniel's expression changed in an instant and he strode to the computer monitor.

"Relax. It's family. Preston's here," Gene said a second later.

"Let him in," Daniel said.

"Do you think he managed to track down the guy who was following us?" Holly asked Daniel.

"We're about to find out," Daniel said, then turned and gave her a quick smile. "No matter what happens, I'll be right there beside you."

She watched him go into the next room, his words still playing in her mind. *Beside her.* That's what he'd said. Not in front of her or behind her.

Daniel, who'd stepped over to the doorway to greet Detective Bowman, never saw her smile.

Chapter Thirteen

Detective Preston Bowman had a booming voice that commanded attention by sheer volume alone. He stood tall, shoulders thrown back, his gaze taking in everything. He seemed as indomitable as a force of nature yet, paradoxically, there was an incredible stillness about him. In this case, Holly suspected it was the calm before the storm.

They'd decided to sit in the area of the main room defined by three-foot walls. As she entered that sitting area, she noted that the brown leather couch and chairs were a matched set.

"Would you like some coffee to warm up?" Daniel asked Preston.

"From the weather outside, or the temperature in here?" he demanded, glancing around. "It feels like a meat locker."

"The thermostat should be up to the mid-sixties by now," Daniel said, going over to check.

"That's a tropical heat wave in here, right?" Preston muttered, then shook his head. "No coffee, I can't stay for long." Bowman looked directly at Holly. "It appears you left a name off the suspect list—Ross Williams."

"It wasn't intentional, Detective," she said. "I hadn't seen Ross for months, and he was so annoying, I guess I blocked him out."

"So who else haven't you thought of?" Preston pressed.

"I can't think of anyone, and I've really tried. You have to understand how things work in my business. My job description requires me to be able to get along with a wide variety of people. Making enemies is counterproductive on every level. I depend heavily on word of mouth to get new clients, too."

"What happened to the guy who followed us into the Bucking Bronco?" Daniel asked. "Did the BOLO get results?"

"Sorry, no. We spoke to Roger Davis, that knuckle dragger you fought. Davis said that some guy in the parking lot handed him fifty bucks to go inside and take you on. His out of focus description told us nothing except that we're dealing with a white male in a baseball cap, something we already knew," Preston said. "It looked to me that Roger had a six-pack too many. Lucky for you. What the hell were you thinking, Dan? He's as big as an ox."

"He was drunk, as you said, and his timing was way off. I knew I'd be okay as long as he didn't get his arms around me."

"He could have squeezed the water out of you." Preston looked back at Holly. "Obviously *someone* wants you dead. Why can't you come up with a name?"

"I don't know!" she said, her voice rising. "I'm not holding anything back."

"Let's get back to *your* responsibility, bro," Daniel snapped. "How did you manage to lose the sedan tailing us? We led him right past you over on Murray Drive."

"Yeah, we screwed up. He crossed over into the mall parking lot. His timing was perfect. The traffic lights changed before our officer could clear the intersection and the subject got away. I was approaching from the west, behind a delivery truck, and lost sight of him for about three minutes. That was all it took for him to disappear among the maybe five-hundred last-minute shoppers on their way in or out of the mall. Then there was the regular go-home crowd."

"Did you send a detective to Ross's home?" Daniel pressed.

"Yeah, sure, but he's supposedly driven on to Winslow for another job fair, and we want to catch him back in the state. We won't quit until we talk to him, but keep in mind we have nothing on Williams except for that incident at the community center, and even then, what do we charge him with? Probability and proof are two different things, and he might just decide to claim *he* was the one being assaulted." Preston glanced at Daniel, who shrugged.

Holly rolled her eyes. "So now what?"

"I'd like you to hang where it's safe until I give you the all clear," Preston said. "Here would be perfect," he said, looking at Daniel.

"How long will that be?" she asked.

"Let's say another hour? After that, things should have calmed down a bit more."

"We'll wait to hear from you," Daniel said.

As Daniel walked out with Preston, discussing what she supposed was a plan, Holly stayed with Gene.

"That's going to be real hard for my brother to do—waiting around for someone else to get answers," Gene said. "Dan's more comfortable taking point and staying in control of the situation."

"I've noticed," she said. "And you?"

"Less so, but the tendency's still there. It comes from having spent way too much of our lives around strangers who decided what was good for us, what we should do and when. These days, turning over the reins to anyone else, even for a moment, doesn't come easy to any of us."

Before she could ask him more, Daniel returned. "I never did feed you dinner," he said, looking at Holly.

"I picked up an extra pizza. It's still in the freezer. Help yourselves," Gene said, waving a hand toward the kitchen.

"Where are you off to?" Daniel asked.

"Unless you need me here, I have to pick up *Hosteen* Silver's death certificate from the mortuary," he said quietly, checking his watch. "We'll need that to file some of the paperwork."

"Go ahead." Daniel stood there silently as Gene left.

"I didn't realize that your foster father had died so recently," Holly said as soon as the door shut.

"About three weeks ago," he said, walking with her across the big room toward the refrigerator. "Gene's handling the paperwork."

"Everything is red tape these days," she said, sympathizing.

"His death took all of us by surprise," Daniel said after a long silence.

"Did he die at home? Is that why Gene isn't staying there?" she asked, wondering why Gene hadn't opted for that, particularly since he hadn't seemed too pleased with the accommodations here at Daniel's.

Of course if *Hosteen* Silver had died at the house, not many Navajos would have felt comfortable there. Fear of the *chindi*, the earthbound and evil side of a man, was believed to remain attached to the place of his death, while the good in him went on to merge with Universal Harmony.

"My foster father went like most Traditionalists. He walked off into the night. I still don't understand why he did that, he wasn't sick, at least as far as we know, but those are the facts," Daniel said. "The reason Gene didn't stay at the house is because he's hoping to find a handyman soon who'll live there while renovating the place."

Daniel found the pizza, wrapped in foil, on top of a stack of frozen dinners. He removed the foil and popped it into the microwave.

"What brand is that?" she asked. "The toppings look so appetizing."

"This isn't store-bought pizza. A Navajo woman makes most of my meals. She gets to raise a little cash that way, and I get great food ready for the microwave. Since Gene's staying here now, she's making extra-large portions. Green chile pizza is his favorite."

"Sounds good to me," she said.

As he waited for the microwave to beep, Daniel took his keys out of his pocket and placed them on the counter. A smaller leather pouch nearly came out along with the keys and he pushed it back down into his pocket.

"That was a medicine bag, wasn't it? I've only seen Traditionalists and New Traditionalists carry those," she said.

"It was a gift from *Hosteen* Silver. He gave one to each of us when we turned seventeen. Inside, among other things, is a fetish. All of my brothers have a different guardian animal, one whose spirit matches him best," Daniel said. "My fetish's spirit is part of what makes me so good in a fight, and why I generally win."

He didn't volunteer any more information and she struggled between respecting his privacy and a nearly overwhelming sense of curiosity. "If you feel I'm prying, don't answer," she said at last, "but I'd like to know which animal he chose for you."

"The badger," he answered, as he removed the pizza from the microwave.

She thought about the qualities that made the animal unique. "When cornered it's a fierce fighter—tenacious and strong. They never give up, no matter what."

He smiled.

"*Hosteen* Silver was right. That does suit you."

After they ate at the little table, they went back to the sitting area. She took a seat on the couch, and Daniel joined her, one arm draped over the back as he faced her. Despite his relaxed pose, she could feel the tension in him.

He glanced at the clock on the wall across the room, looked at his cell phone, then back at her. "Can you think of a good way for us to pass the time?" he asked, a slow smile spreading over his face.

For a brief second she fought the impulse to lie against that wonderfully broad chest and hide in the shelter of his arms.

Holly clamped down on the thought almost as soon as it formed. *Was she crazy?* What they had was a temporary arrangement, that was all. She knew only too well how men changed, how undependable they could become. Her father had been a prime example. That was why she'd fought so hard to make herself strong—to have the ability to stand on her own.

"Actually, I do have an idea," she said at length, focusing on the real reason they were together. "Teach me that nerve pinch you used to control Ross Williams."

For a second she was almost sure she saw disappointment flash in his eyes. Annoyed with herself for what she suspected was the product of her overactive imagination, she stared at her lap, steadied herself, then added, "I don't like feeling helpless."

"I hear you."

His words resonated with an emotion she couldn't identify at first. Then, recalling what Gene had said about their days in foster care, Holly realized that Daniel probably did understand exactly how she felt.

He took her hand, then pressed the center and back of her palm. "There's a nerve here, and if you apply enough pressure with your thumb you can bring a man to his knees. But it's not a good technique for a woman who has no training. You'd need to get in too close and your best defense is distance. If you're standing, you know kicking a man in the groin will buy you a few seconds to make tracks. You might also consider carrying a can of mace."

"That means reaching into my purse and hoping I can find it fast during a crisis situation. All things considered, I'm more likely to end up spraying myself."

He laughed, but before he could say anything else, the telephone rang. Daniel answered it on the first ring, then put the call on the speaker.

"I spoke to Williams. He never made it out of the state because of a storm front near Flagstaff," Bowman said. "He claimed that he was at the Turquoise Bar the night Holly was attacked outside the café. At first I figured he was trying to snow me. The place is a zoo even on weeknights and verifying that alibi would have been nearly impossible. Then he told me that he'd had a problem with the bartender that night. He hit on one of the waitresses and it turned out to be the guy's daughter. I verified it and Williams was there."

"So if it wasn't Ross, then who's after me?" Holly said, fear tightening its grip on her.

"You tell me. Keep thinking about it."

After the call ended, Daniel looked over at her. "You're shaking like a leaf," he said, and pulled her into his arms. "You don't have to be afraid, Holly. He's not going to win."

His words and the warmth of his embrace comforted her, but as her fear subsided, she eased out of his arms. Though Daniel made it easy, she couldn't allow herself to cling to anyone. Fear was a cruel enemy. It didn't attack when you could easily defeat it. It lay in wait, and caught you unawares when you were most vulnerable. Daniel was a dependable ally, but fear came from within, and that was a battle she'd have to fight and win alone.

"As a kid, I learned to survive by quieting the voice inside me that said I wasn't strong enough, or brave enough to do what had to be done," she said. "I refused to listen, particularly when it told me that I'd never be able to get what I wanted most out of life."

"What is it that you're after, Holly?"

"The same thing most women value. Life defined by love, the kind that's steady and sure, come rain or shine."

"Neither life nor love is that perfect."

"Maybe not, but it'll be real enough for me when I find it."

"It's easier to live in the moment. What do you want right now?" Daniel asked, his gaze holding hers.

The storm raging in his eyes ignited a fire that swept through her, yet she knew that what he was offering was only temporary. Halfway propositions and empty promises had defined her life growing up. She wouldn't settle for that ever again.

"I'm not the kind who lives just for today, Daniel."

"Learning to live for the moment can give you a very sweet sense of freedom," he said.

"That depends on how you define freedom. I find it by choosing my own destiny." She stood and put more distance between them. "So is it safe for me to go home now?"

"Yeah, I'll drive you back, check your place out, then take off. Tomorrow we'll get a fresh start. Do you have anything special coming up in your schedule?"

"I'll need to check in with Martin, but there's nothing for tomorrow that I know about yet. I have upcoming presentations I'll need to work on at the office, but you don't have to babysit me constantly. Maybe you could set up some cameras. That should do the trick."

"My job is to keep you safe. I can't guarantee that if I'm not there."

"Let's see how things play out, then. Maybe Detective Bowman will turn up something later tonight."

"Is there a reason why you don't want me around?" he asked, getting right to the point.

Holly hesitated, trying to figure out how to answer him. The truth was, her attraction to Daniel scared her because she knew it could only lead to trouble. He was the wrong kind of man for her. He liked danger and adventure and she wanted a quiet, predictable life.

Miss Caution and Mr. Reckless. No way it could work. She had to accept that and move on. Yet when she looked at him, all common sense went out the window. She wanted him to kiss her again, to make her feel as if she were melting inside, and needing things she didn't even dare name.

Chapter Fourteen

He was uneasy sitting this close to Holly in the confines of his SUV. As it had been on the sofa just a while ago, her scent teased him. All he wanted to do right now was pull over and kiss her senseless.

He kept his gaze on the road, his face rigid. He had a job to do, and he'd have to keep it strictly business. That was the only way they'd get through this without the kind of scars that would last a lifetime.

He could offer her a night of passion and take her on a journey of pleasure that would light up even the darkest sky. Yet for him, it would go no further than that.

He'd end up hurting Holly, and that was the last thing he wanted to do. What she wanted—the kind of man who'd go to work at eight and return home promptly at five—just wasn't him.

Women—they were trouble no matter how you looked at it. "When we get to your house, stay close until we're inside. Like before, wait by the door while I check out the place. If there's trouble, run back out here and call 911. Got it?"

"Do you think he's waiting for me?"

He heard the tremor in her voice and saw her swallow hard. He cursed himself for being so blunt. "No. It's unlikely that anyone's broken in. It's just procedure, part of a checklist."

"Then why are *you* so tense?" she asked.

The fact that she could read his mood took him by surprise.

No one usually could, except for Preston. "What makes you think I'm tense?"

"You set your jaw, and your eyes…get hard."

"Right now, I'm trying to anticipate this guy's next move. I want to be able to counter whatever he throws at us. He's skilled but also reckless, or maybe desperate. I'm not sure."

"I don't understand any of this," she said, running an exasperated hand through her hair. "Why me? It takes a lot of hatred to want anyone dead. How can I have made someone so angry and not know it?"

"It may not be anger or hatred. It could be about power, or maybe he's trying to neutralize a person he sees as a threat. You haven't witnessed a crime, have you?"

"If I had, don't you think I would have remembered?" She shuddered. "I wish I had some of your toughness and could look at things stone cold."

"Toughness is a label that belongs to anyone who refuses to give up. You've done just fine. You've proven that you can think fast and stand up for yourself."

Soon they arrived at her home in Hartley. Daniel covered her back as she unlocked the front door, then he went inside first. Signaling her to wait, he walked quickly through her home, checking out the other rooms and looking into the backyard via the windows. As soon as he was satisfied that everything was as it should be, he rejoined her in the living room.

"It's okay."

"Good. Now I can breathe again," she said.

"What time do you want me to pick you up tomorrow?"

"Seven," she said.

"I'll be here."

Daniel was heading to the door when he heard a metallic noise on the front porch, then a clank. Reaching for Holly, he pulled her to the floor.

"Stay down." Daniel drew his weapon, then moved toward

the door. Staying low, he reached up, turned the handle and pulled hard. The door moved less than an inch.

"Something's attached to the door on the outside, holding it shut," he said. "Head for the kitchen. Hurry."

"What's that smell?" she asked, curling her nose.

"Smoke. Move fast!"

As they rushed through the dining room and into the kitchen, smoke was already seeping into the house from around the overhead light fixtures. A smoke alarm in the hall began its high-pitched electronic beep and the acrid scent of burning wood permeated the air.

As soon as they reached the back door, he reached for the knob, but it refused to turn at all. He checked the dead bolt, but it wouldn't turn, either. "It's either jammed or glued shut. I can't get the mechanism to work." He kicked the knob, bending it a little, then tried again. It wouldn't budge.

Daniel glanced back at her, expecting Holly to be close to panic. Instead he found that she'd pulled a chair over to the sink, and was fighting to open the kitchen window.

"This danged thing won't budge, either," she said, thumping the wood with the heel of her hand.

"Get back. I'm going to break it out." Daniel picked up the small microwave oven from the kitchen counter, unplugged the cord, then threw the appliance into the glass. The window shattered as the oven flew outside. The opening was now big enough for them to crawl through. Daniel grabbed an oven mitt from a cup hook on the cabinet and started to break away the slivers of glass that still clung to the frame.

Before he could finish the job, a gunshot shook the house and a bullet whistled past his ear, striking the wall behind him. He ducked away, grabbed Holly and pushed her to the floor. The room was already so full of smoke it was like moving through a toxic fog.

"There's a fire in the attic and we're trapped. He's won,"

she said, her voice breaking. "Either he shoots us or we burn to death."

"He won't be able to stick around much longer. Others will hear the gunshot, and once people look outside or smell smoke, they'll call for help. Police and fire trucks will respond and the area will be filled with people. He has to take off and we have to stay alive long enough for help to reach us."

As Holly started to cough, Daniel grabbed a hand towel from the kitchen island, wet it under the sink faucet, then handed it to her. "Breathe through this, and stay as close to the floor as you can. Smoke rises."

He found a dishcloth, then soaked it for himself. Once back on the floor beside Holly, he studied the interior as far as he could see. The gray smoke seemed thickest around the den. They'd have to avoid that section.

"I'm for getting out of here. Let's go try a bedroom window," he said.

"Hallway, to the left."

They worked their way toward the front of the house, crouching as low as they could. As they went past a doorway, he turned his head to check on Holly. Before he could stop her, she ducked into the living room, reached for something on the top shelf of the bookcase and stuck it in her jacket pocket.

"No! Don't try to salvage anything now. Focus on getting out of here," Daniel yelled.

A coughing spasm made him realize how thick and toxic the air was now. He continued moving, now on his hands and knees, the moist dish towel tied around his face, protecting his lungs. As he made his way down the hall, he felt a rough grid against his knees and looked down. "You've got a floor furnace," he said.

"Yeah."

"Help me lift the register," he said. "If we can slip down into the crawl space, we can get away from the heat and smoke."

"What if the heater comes on? We'll be roasted."

Daniel coughed, then with effort forced himself to stop. It was getting hot and the smoke was building to dangerous levels. "No choice," he yelled, trying to be heard over the din of the smoke alarm on the ceiling overhead. "Fire's blocking the way forward," he said, shifting and letting her see the flames ahead along the wall where curtains had ignited.

Daniel focused on the metal grill, checking for possible hinges, then stuck his fingers in the grid and yanked. The large, rectangular metal cover came completely loose. Below, he could see the old-school pilot light by one of the burners.

"Can you squeeze down on the left side?" he asked, pointing into the hole.

"I think I can wiggle through." Holly scooted over, dropping her legs over the edge. "How far down before I reach the ground?"

Daniel could now see flames coming from the kitchen and living room. "Doesn't matter. Work your way down fast, then grab on to anything that looks solid."

Slipping around the metal structure, she wriggled down into the darkness.

"My turn," Daniel said as something crashed to the floor in the next room and flames flared out along the floor, extending into the hall.

Daniel brushed past the warm metal furnace and felt the tip of his boots touch soft dirt. Ducking down, he inched along the ground in a deep crouch.

The air wasn't bad here except for the strong scent of dust and dirt. Ahead, he could see Holly on her knees beside a concrete foundation pillar. The heavy floor beams were covered in cobwebs and the entire crawl space smelled funky and damp, but they could breathe.

"I'm turned around down here," she called out. "Which way to the back of the house?"

Daniel studied the plumbing as he inched over beside her. "That way," he said, pointing. "Why?"

"That's where the crawl space door is," Holly said. "Do you think he nailed or glued it shut?"

"Even if he did, I can probably kick that open," Daniel said.

There was a loud crash, then sparks and flames erupted as part of the floor broke through, bringing something down into the crawl space with them.

"My old wardrobe." Holly tried to swallow back her tears. "The fire's destroying everything I love."

"It'll take us, too, unless we get out of here before the gas line ruptures. Head for the back wall."

The glow of the fire now illuminated their way. Fifteen seconds later, on hands and knees, they stopped by the small door, barely three-feet wide and two-feet high. Daniel pushed against it, but it didn't move.

Muttering an oath, he brought up his knees and kicked hard near the left edge of the door. It swung open, revealing two pink slippers attached to a pair of legs.

"Here she is!" a woman cried out. "Help! Over here!"

"Lois, my next door neighbor," Holly told Daniel, taking the hand the woman offered.

FIREMEN WERE ALREADY PULLING up when Holly and Daniel reached the front yard. One of her neighbors had broken the window on Holly's old pickup and rolled the vehicle out into the street, so it hadn't burned along with the house.

Daniel's SUV, parked along the curb, was also untouched. EMTs checked them out for smoke inhalation, then pronounced them lucky, and in good shape.

Holly stood back in the street, looking at the still-blazing pile of rubble that had once been her home. The only recognizable feature that remained intact was the brick chimney, and it glowed from the intense heat. She swallowed hard, sure she was going to be sick.

As a kid, she'd repeatedly lost the things she loved every time she and her dad had left town—usually in the dead of night. Her father's love of gambling had invariably brought enemies to their doorstep, and if not that, then bill collectors or court clerks carrying a summons.

She'd made her own home into a fortress of sorts, filling it with treasures she'd believed would never be taken away from her, but fate was having the last laugh. As she watched helplessly, fire stripped her of everything that had defined her. Only one small keepsake remained, what she'd managed to pluck off the shelf at the last minute.

As the flames slowly receded, Holly felt as if a piece of her were disappearing along with the thin gray smoke that rose upward into the dark sky. Though her heart was breaking, she couldn't take her eyes off the glowing embers the fire hoses had yet to quench.

Daniel came to stand beside her, and placed his arm over her shoulders. "You can rebuild the house, Holly. It'll be a new beginning for you."

"I've had too many of those fresh starts, and experience doesn't make it any easier," she said, giving him a thin smile.

"What was it that you stopped to get out of the living room?" he asked.

"A piece of my past, something I would never be able to replace."

Before Daniel could ask what it was, Preston joined them. He looked at Daniel, then at Holly. "You two look like hell, but I'm glad you're okay," he said bluntly. "What happened?"

Daniel gave him the highlights, suggesting that his brother work with the fire marshal to determine why they couldn't open either door. "Someone in the neighborhood may have seen whoever did that," Daniel said.

"I'll handle it. Did either of you get a look at your assailant?" Preston asked.

Holly shook her head. "Not me."

"This wasn't an in-your-face type of attack," Daniel said. "He set a trap, then waited. We never saw him."

"Is it possible Ross…" Holly asked, leaving the question hanging.

"No. We've had an officer watching his place. He never left," Preston said.

"So we're back to square one," Daniel said.

"Less than that," Holly said. "At square one I had a home."

"Find a place to stay," Preston said, "but avoid any location that's logical to anyone who knows anything about you."

"My place is well guarded," Daniel said.

Preston shook his head. "If he knew where she lived, it's more than likely he knows all about you, too. Give me some time to get manpower in place around your office and set up some patrols in that area before you take her back there. I'll need till morning, at least."

"I hate motels," Holly said, her voice flat and far away as she remembered days long past.

"Think of something," Preston said. "Meanwhile, while you two hole up, I'll talk to everyone here. Do you think any of your neighbors have security cameras?" he asked, looking around.

Holly gave him an exhausted, sad smile. "Probably not. This has always been a quiet neighborhood. Trouble here was usually limited to Mrs. Sanchez's tomcat, and his forays into Mr. Goldberg's greenhouse. We do have one well-meaning busybody who's always watching out her window. Mrs. Harris might be able to help you. I hear she's even got a telescope."

"Where does she live?" Preston asked.

Holly pointed down the block. "Three houses down, but if she'd seen anyone hanging around, like the guy who tampered with the back door and windows, she would have called your department in a flash."

"I'll speak to her. In the meantime, lay low until you hear from me," Preston said.

Daniel nodded once, then led Holly back to his SUV. He'd moved it to make room for a fire truck.

"You hate this as much as I do," she said, noting Daniel's grim expression as they set out. "You want to go on the offensive and draw him out."

"Yeah, I do, but my assignment is to keep you safe."

"I won't be safe as long as he's out there. He's taken my home, and if he keeps this up, he'll make it impossible for me to continue my work. My company will fold, and then I'll have nothing left. I need to fight him now before he ruins my life completely."

"When you fight an opponent like this one, both sides get bloody. It's a dirty business," he said, pulling away.

"He's destroying me one piece at a time. I've got to strike back." Her voice broke, and she fell silent. "What this man has taken from me is more than just my house. It was the home I loved. Living there also made me part of that wonderful neighborhood. I'd made a place for myself there. Now everything's changed."

As a foster kid who'd never belonged anywhere until *Hosteen* Silver took him in, he understood the need to carve out a place for yourself. "It might seem almost impossible to you now, but you'll recover from this."

"Not as long as he remains out there, waiting." She took a slow, deep breath. "I want my life back, and that means we need to come up with a plan to catch him."

"He'll find out pretty soon that we're both alive and well. Then he'll come after us again. That's when we'll make our move," Daniel said. "It's all about strategy and timing."

Holly leaned back into her seat as they headed down the highway. "So where to now?"

"Deep into the Rez."

"What if we're tailed?"

"We haven't been," he said. "I've kept an eye out."

He made a sudden right turn that left her grabbing for the door handle to keep her balance. "Hey—"

"Just making sure." He looked in the rearview mirror again. "Nope. No one there."

Daniel had an unshakable confidence, and from what she'd seen so far, it wasn't misplaced. She wished she could have given him and Preston more help. "This man always comes at me out of nowhere. I wish I could figure out who he is so I can end this once and for all."

"What we have to do next is go back to our original question—how and why he targeted you. I want you to expand that list of suspects by considering people you only have limited contact with, like a grocery clerk, for example. What kind of things do you do on a regular schedule? Think of all your activities throughout the course of a week."

"I go grocery shopping on Monday. Tuesdays I get gas. Wednesdays and Thursdays I work late at the office. Fridays and Saturdays I usually stay home. Sundays I have dinner at Simple Pleasures, and go for a walk around the neighborhood, talk to my neighbors, maybe go to our neighborhood association meeting. Afterward, I head home."

"Always on the same days?"

"Yes. I tend to follow set schedules. That's why I get everything done."

"While I keep driving, call Preston and tell him what you just told me."

She dialed the number Daniel had on speed dial and gave the detective the information, then she called her insurance company. At least she'd had the foresight to keep a copy of all her important papers in her office safe.

When she ended the calls, she looked around and saw that they were heading west. They'd gone past the turnoff to the natural gas plant and were traveling even farther into the Navajo Nation. "How deep into the Rez are we going? Remember that I have to meet Martin early tomorrow. I need my job more than ever now, and I can't afford to give him any reasons to start searching for a replacement."

"One thing at a time. We need to get through tonight first."

The reality of his words hit her hard. She swallowed and said nothing. Reaching into her purse, she felt for the one treasure she'd saved. It was all she had, but it reminded her of how far she'd come.

"When you're up against an enemy like this one, you need two things. One is endurance, and the other's patience," he said. "He'll pay for what he's done, Holly. That's a guarantee."

Though she knew he was as good as his word, the fear in her heart remained. There was more than one kind of danger ahead. To trust, to hope.... That left you too open and vulnerable in a world that favored the strong.

Chapter Fifteen

Although the drive continued to take them farther west into the reservation, and they were now driving up a dirt road in the foothills, she hadn't asked him again where he was headed. Daniel had respected her privacy by not pressuring her to tell him what she'd salvaged from her home. Now it was her turn. Honoring the Navajo sense of balance, she showed her trust in him by her silence.

"Okay, go ahead and ask." His voice was low and deep, and echoed with that ever-present hint of danger. "I know you want to know where I'm going. And don't worry. I won't press you for information about what you took out of your home."

"The two things are completely different. Our location impacts both of us because knowing where I am may help determine my survival. What I took...." She left it hanging.

"Is personal?" he said, finishing the thought for her. "Then the two things aren't as different as you might think. You'll understand once we get there," he said. Moments later, he pointed ahead. "The moon's out, so once we round the bend, you'll see it."

"It's a log cabin," she said, leaning forward, struggling to catch a glimpse through the pines.

"Yes. That's where we lived the first year we stayed with *Hosteen* Silver."

As they completed the turn, the place came into full view, resting against a hill. "It looks very small, particularly for three men."

"It is, and when we first arrived, there was no running water inside. Gene and I had to carry it uphill two buckets at a time from the well down in a hollow. Let me tell you, for two city kids, that seemed like torture."

"I gather you two didn't warm up to *Hosteen* Silver right away?"

He laughed. "He scared the hell out of both of us, and keep in mind that we came from tough backgrounds. That man had a stare that could drill holes into you, and, well, that *hataalii* stuff…. We both saw him do things…." He shook his head. "I'd tell you, but you'd think I was nuts—and I wouldn't blame you."

"I've worked for your tribe for years and have met many interesting people. I won't judge. Just because I can't explain it doesn't mean it isn't valid or real."

He considered it, then nodded. "*Hosteen* Silver was a healer, but he had another talent, too. He sometimes knew things *before* they happened. When he told you something good—or bad—was coming, it would happen as he said."

"That's an amazing gift," she said.

He nodded slowly. "He could stargaze, something not all *hataaliis* can do. He'd stare at a crystal or at the sky and see things no one else could. Yet most of the time he'd refuse to tell us what he saw because he didn't want to clear the path ahead for us. He believed that the ability to meet a challenge was the real measure of a man."

"He sounds like a remarkable person. I wish I'd have known him."

"I think he would have liked you," Daniel said.

She couldn't help but smile. "Why, because I keep an open mind?"

He shook his head. "No, because you have the strength to take whatever life throws at you. Losing your home cut you to the bone and I know you're hurting inside, but you refuse to fall apart."

"Do you want to know what really gets to me about all this? It was my father's lifestyle that attracted this kind of trouble, not mine. I've spent my entire adult life playing by different rules. I don't understand why or how violence found me."

"The *Diné* believe that good and evil coexist, each keeping the other in check. You can't escape either, because both are a part of life."

A moment later Daniel parked in front of the wood cabin. "Let's go. This late at night, and at this altitude, it's extremely cold, so we need to get inside. It's not five-star lodging, but these days it does have running water. Mind you, there's no *hot* water, but you can heat it in the wood-and-coal stove."

He led the way to the front door, then glanced back at her. "I almost forgot to tell you, we might also have a houseguest."

"Who?"

"Not who, what," he answered.

As they went inside, he signaled her to be quiet and listened. "He's here," he said.

She looked at him, and stayed perfectly still, waiting.

"My brother and I came up here after *Hosteen* Silver passed away just to look things over. Gene caught a glimpse of an animal underneath the brush near the back door, so he made a loud noise hoping to run it off, but the animal didn't leave. Instead it came out to face him. It was a badger, probably from a big meadow not far from here."

"They're tough and won't generally back off. Did he try to attack Gene?"

"No, nothing like that. Gene has…a way with animals. He saw that there was something wrong with the badger's hind leg, so the animal couldn't run. Since the badger is my spiritual brother, and there was a snowstorm coming, we opened the back door that leads into the mudroom. At first it was reluctant to go inside, but as I said, Gene has a gift."

Daniel's eyes shone as he continued the story.

"While he took care of the injured leg, I turned over a cardboard box so it looked like a den, and placed some old blankets inside it. The badger came in, and took up residence there. His injured leg has apparently healed, but he's decided to stick around. He comes and goes through a doggie door-like opening Gene made for it, and makes a meal out of any rodents that come into the house. The arrangement is balanced. It works for him and for us."

"Badgers serve a purpose in nature, keeping the rodent population down for one," she said, "but they *don't* make good pets."

"He isn't one. He comes and goes as he pleases and, in return for shelter, he provides a service. If you leave him alone, he'll do the same for you. Just don't corner him."

As they entered the living room, Daniel picked up some fragments of wood stacked in a metal box next to the fireplace and began to make a fire. "This kindling is rich in sap. We keep it handy so we can get a fire going in a hurry. The room warms up quickly, too. That was the best part of living in a house this small."

Holly heard a scuttling noise and, as she turned her head, saw the badger peering at them through an opening at floor level in a rear door. She made sure not to look directly at it, something the animal might misinterpret as aggression, and soon the badger backed out and disappeared from view.

"It won't come into this room," Daniel said.

"How can you be so sure?"

"After *Hosteen* Silver gave Gene his medicine bundle, Gene discovered that he could communicate with animals. Not talk to them, mind you. It's more like an understanding that exists between him and them. Gene assured me that the badger will respect my space because he knows that there's a link between his spirit and mine," Daniel said. "I don't really know about all that, but I can tell you this—I don't feel threatened by the badger, nor he by me."

"And you? What's your gift?" she asked after a moment's pause.

"Like badger, I can sense danger. I've been able to use that in the work I do and help others guard whatever needs to be protected."

"Like me."

"Your enemy is now mine."

His words reverberated with power and conviction, pushing her fears back into the dark recesses of her mind. "I hate violence of any kind," she said, her voice whisper soft. "To be drawn into this fight and not even know why makes me crazy inside."

"Even in battle, we can walk in beauty." He pressed his palm to the side of her face, his thumb leaving a gentle caress there. "Remember that."

As she looked into his eyes, she almost forgot to breathe. There was a gentle protectiveness there that had never been part of her life. It made her ache and long for more.

As the fire crackled and popped from the resin-rich piñon firewood, the spell was broken.

"My brother and I keep supplies here in case of emergency," he said, turning away. "There are canned soups, beans and even stew in the cupboard. Would you like something to eat?"

"Thanks, but no. I'm not hungry. It's very late and I should be exhausted, but I'm too tense to even sleep."

"If Preston identifies the man who's after you, he'll call me right away. We get phone service here because we're at the high end of the canyon and in line with a cell tower in the valley."

"Your brother has probably called it a night already," she said, aware that it was close to two in the morning.

Daniel shook his head. "I doubt that. Preston lives and breathes his job. He considers having a predator operating on his turf a personal affront. He won't rest until the guy's behind bars."

"I've seen that kind of dedication before," she said quietly.

She wondered if that kind of solitary existence was what the future held for her, too. She'd spent years not letting anyone get too close. Eventually, she'd hoped to find an undemanding, predictable and dependable man to share her life with, though as she thought about it now, it suddenly sounded terribly boring.

"My brother and I started our new lives in this cabin. Once the man after you is caught, you're welcome to stay here until your home is ready for you to settle into again."

"Thanks, but I was thinking of moving into my office in Hartley. I hate the thought of spending Christmas away from everything that's familiar to me."

"Are you sure you're okay?" he asked, hearing her voice tremble.

She hadn't meant to, but suddenly her tears started flowing and she couldn't stop crying. "My life was so organized and simple! I was meeting my goals every day and I knew exactly where I was headed. Now I don't even recognize myself."

He crossed the room and pulled her into his arms. "Take things one step at a time."

As Daniel held her tightly against him, her tears slowly subsided. She never wanted to leave that wonderful circle of protection, but other yearnings soon rose to tempt her as she burrowed into him. She knew then that it was time for her to move away, but she didn't want to, not just yet.

"I know what it's like to feel all alone, but you're not, Holly. Don't you know that?" he murmured in her ear. "I'm here for you."

His words touched her heart. "I don't want to be afraid anymore," she whispered.

"You don't have to be," he said, tightening his hold.

She could feel every part of him pressed against her. She wanted to lose herself in that heat…or maybe find herself there. Aware of the force of her own longing, and worried about where it might lead her, she stepped away.

Avoiding his gaze, Holly moved to the soft sheepskin rug

in front of the fireplace and sat down. "Tell me more about yourself, Daniel. I know so little about you."

"You're uncomfortable trusting someone who's still mostly a stranger to you," he said with a nod.

"I'd like to be your friend, but that takes knowing you as more than just a kind almost-stranger who came to rescue me. Tell me where you came from. Where did you live before *Hosteen* Silver took you into his family?"

He sat next to her beside the fire. "My mother was a waitress at an Albuquerque bar and my dad was a Navajo man she met one night. I never knew much more than that. I don't think she did, either. It didn't really matter, because my mom and I were close and always there for each other. Then one night she didn't come home. I waited, and a couple of days later, the police and child services came to the door." He paused, his jaw set, his gaze on the flames. "That's when I learned that there'd been a fight at the bar, and a stray bullet had taken her life. I'd just turned twelve."

"You must have been terrified, so young and suddenly alone," she said, reaching for his hand.

"I was afraid, but the worst of it was the loneliness. I missed her." He paused as her fingers entwined with his.

"You had no other relatives?"

"Not that I knew about, and no one came forward. My mother had left the Navajo Nation when she was sixteen and never went back. She'd hated living in poverty and had seen her sister and father die of cancer. She believed it had been the result of drinking polluted water—a legacy of the uranium mines," Daniel said. "She worked hard, and made a life for herself and eventually me, in Albuquerque."

"After she was gone, did they try to place you with a Navajo family?" she asked.

"I'm not sure. All I can tell you is that I was first taken to live with an Anglo couple in the south valley. At the time I was so sad I didn't care where they sent me. I never realized how rough things would get for me."

"You didn't like the family?"

"I always had the feeling they just wanted able bodies who could work on their farm and that's why they'd taken in five boys. For me, the real problem was the gangs around there and at school. They didn't like anyone who stood up to them. Their idea of a fair fight was six against one, so I kept getting beat up. Eventually, I was sent to live with another family, then another. Being the new kid on the block meant always proving yourself, so I became one badass kid."

"Yes, but it was out of necessity, not choice."

He gave her a gentle smile as he stroked her hand with his thumb. "No one ever bothered to see that. I was labeled a high-risk kid."

As Daniel spoke, Holly could see the toll those memories took on him. He'd tried to bury them, but there was no hole deep enough to erase the echoes of pain. Even a strong heart could bleed.

"Trouble and I became allies. I was told that I was no good so many times, I started to live up to the label. By the time I turned fourteen I'd ended up in a boot camp-like foster home with four other boys, two of them on probation. That's where I met Gene. He's as big as I am now, but back then, he was a runt. The other guys picked on both of us because we were different—Indians. I had to watch his back or they would have put him in the hospital."

"How did Gene end up there?"

He shook his head. "I can tell you about myself, but *Hosteen* Silver taught us that one Navajo doesn't speak for another. In this case, it's even more so. My brother has his own secrets."

"You're right. I'm sorry," she said. "Why don't you tell me how you met *Hosteen* Silver?"

"His niece worked for the foster care system and told him about me and Gene. He came to the house a few weeks after that. He and I spoke for hours. He wasn't put off by my attitude at all, and that confused the heck out of me. Then he told me that he wanted me to go live with him."

"How did you feel about that?" she asked, eager to know more about Daniel.

"I told him the truth. I wouldn't have minded going some-place new, but my mother hadn't been happy on the Rez and I didn't want to go back there, either."

"But he took you anyway?"

He shook his head. "He never forced anything. That wasn't his way. *Hosteen* Silver always presented you with choices, then let you make up your own mind. In my case, he pointed out that if I stayed on the path I was traveling, I'd end up in the detention home or prison. Then he told me that if I were sent away for any reason at all, Gene's chances of staying in one piece were slim. Gene was a sickly kid back then and he was a magnet for bullies."

"He'd spoken to Gene?"

"Not yet, but he'd done his homework. He'd intended all along on taking both of us, but he started with me, figuring I could sway Gene. It worked, and that's how we ended up at this house."

"Wow. That's amazing. I have a feeling that when *Hosteen* Silver made up his mind nothing stood in his way."

"True enough," he said. "To the world, Gene and I were trouble and not worth anyone's time. He saw two lonely kids who had to be tough so that life wouldn't destroy what was left of them."

"I know what it's like to try and hide from the world," she said. "There was a time in my life when we lived mostly on the run."

"You grew up with your dad, right?"

"My mother had a bad heart, but by the time we found out, it was too late. One night when I was seven, she passed out in the kitchen. She went into the hospital, but there was nothing anyone could do." She stopped and swallowed hard. "After that, it was just Dad and me. He tried to be a good father, but gambling owned him after he lost his day job, and there was little room in his heart for anything, or anyone, else."

She reached for her handbag, still on the chair. "I can't tell you how many times he and I had to take off in the middle of the night, leaving everything we owned behind. Eventually I started keeping my clothes in a suitcase. Time and again I'd lose the things I loved—all except for one. It was a gift from my mother and I kept it with me no matter where I went." She pulled out a battered-looking six-inch teddy bear from her purse. "This is the only thing I've ever managed to keep. It smells like smoke now, but it doesn't matter. It's priceless to me."

He pulled her against him. "Holding on…it's what people like us do best."

He lowered his mouth to hers and was about to kiss her when the front door flew open. Instantly Daniel whirled around, gun in hand.

"Whoa! It's me, bro!" Gene said. "After I spoke to Preston, I knew exactly where you'd gone. I've come with extra food and blankets. It's starting to snow and blow out there."

"Thank you, Gene. That was very thoughtful of you," Holly stammered, her heart still at her throat.

Daniel glared at his brother a moment longer, his eyes fixed. "Next time you decide to drop in, honk the horn, call out or something, will you?"

Gene set two large grocery bags onto the couch, then brushed snow off his shoulders. "Don't hold back, Dan," he said with an irrepressible grin. "I know you're overwhelmed by my kindness and overjoyed to see me again." As he glanced at Holly, then at his brother, his expression suddenly changed. "Uh…did I interrupt something? I can hit the trail now— slipping and sliding all the way."

"Shut the door before we all freeze to death," Daniel

growled. "If it's really that bad outside, you should probably stay till morning—which is only a few hours away now."

Gene walked to the window and stood to one side, looking outside. "I know what Preston told you, but I still think you would have been safer at your office, bro. This storm is going to pass through pretty fast, but right now it looks like we're in for whiteout conditions. We may be snowbound for a while."

"Just the three of us. Terrific," Daniel muttered, standing behind him.

Gene laughed. "At least I brought fresh coffee and plenty of food."

"You made sure you weren't tailed, right?"

"No one tailed me, bro, you know better than to ask. I've got a sixth sense that tells me when I'm being watched. That's what kept me alive growing up. I got even better at it after *Hosteen* Silver taught me about tracking and hunting. No one sneaks up on me."

Daniel nodded. "I hear you, but how about going out there anyway and taking a look around before any tracks get covered by the snow."

"You're thinking that someone besides me might have figured out where you went?"

Daniel nodded. "The thought occurred to me."

"Let me get my rifle from the truck first," Gene said, "then I'll take a walk down the road."

Holly watched Gene leave. "This is turning out to be the worst Christmas holiday season ever—and, for me, that's saying a lot."

"Don't give up on Christmas yet. A lot can happen in four days."

As he kissed her lightly, Holly suppressed a shiver. More than anything, she wished she could peer into her own future and see if Daniel would be there, too.

Daniel looked out the window and Holly went to stand beside him. The snow had stopped for a moment, and through a break in the clouds, she saw the faint glimmer of a star shining brightly somewhere beyond Copper Canyon. As she'd done as a child, she wished upon that bright star, knowing there was no better time for hope than the season of miracles.

Chapter Sixteen

Shortly after daybreak, Holly woke up to the roar of an engine. She sat up, struggling to come awake and shrug off the tangle of blankets that covered her.

"What time is it?" she muttered, looking around.

They'd all slept on foam sleeping pads next to the small fireplace. The guys had assured her that it was best to stay together in case of trouble, but she suspected that they, too, had wanted to stay close to the only source of heat. While she didn't see a thermometer, she guessed the temperature inside the cabin was close to freezing.

Holly wrapped one of the blankets around her as she stood and glanced around. Somehow, she'd ended up with almost all the covers. "We each had three blankets when I fell asleep. What happened? How did I end up with, what, eight of them?" she asked Daniel, who was placing wood on the fire.

"My brother found a sleeping bag that was still useable in a trunk, so he didn't need any," Daniel said.

"And you?"

"I had my coat," Daniel answered. "That and one blanket was enough."

"Oh, wow," she said in a whisper. "You froze so I could be warm? Guilt, *major* guilt!"

He laughed. "I stayed close to the fire, and my coat is very warm." He stoked the flames, then glanced back at her. "But if you really feel guilty, I can come up with some fun ways you can make it up to me."

"Nah, never mind. Now that I've had a chance to think about it, I don't feel *that* guilty after all," she said, laughing.

"Guys, I'm heading back," Gene said, as he came in from outside.

"Close that door!" Daniel yelled.

"I was getting to it," Gene said, stomping snow off his boots. "My truck's warmed up now so I'm taking off. I have to meet the tribal attorney who's helping me get our foster father's papers in order. I'll give you a call on my way back to town and let you know about the road conditions."

Holly looked out the window. "We're practically snowed in," she said. "You're not going to make it to the road."

"It's not that bad, only about four-inches deep. Besides, I've got snow tires, and chains if I need them. That pickup of mine sees worse when I head out to feed livestock in the winter. Of course I'm sure my brother will want to stay here awhile longer before heading out. He's sensitive to the cold and more... delicate."

"That'll cost you later," Daniel growled.

Gene laughed, then good to his word, said goodbye and left. Holly heard him slowly drive away a few minutes later, his truck in low gear.

"We've got some five-minute oatmeal in the kitchen," Daniel said, motioning toward the other room. "I've also got a fire going in the stove. We can boil water for that and get some coffee brewing, too."

"Sounds good. Let me help," she said.

Ten minutes later the oatmeal was done, and she spooned it into two bowls. Gene had brought a quart of milk, which made the oatmeal more palatable than with the powdered stuff she'd found in the cabinet.

"If I haven't heard from Preston by the time we finish breakfast, I'll call him," Daniel said, and poured the coffee into two mugs.

As Holly walked over to the small table, she heard the scuttle of the badger in the next room. "The cold temperatures should keep him quiet. They don't hibernate, but they slow down considerably," she said. "Do you ever feed him?"

"We did while he was injured, and we left water out for him, but now that he's well he takes care of himself."

She nodded, thinking how much like the badger Daniel was. He had his own streak of wildness. As her gaze strayed over his shoulders, she remembered how hard and muscular his body was, and how wonderful it had felt to be in his arms.

"What's on your mind?" he asked, adding a teaspoon of sugar to his oatmeal.

Realizing that she'd been staring, she looked down at her cereal, then gave it a stir. "Just waiting for the sugar and thinking of the badger," she mumbled.

"No you weren't," he answered with a ghost of a smile.

"Aw, be quiet," she snapped.

He laughed.

Several minutes later, finished with breakfast, Daniel reached for his cell phone. He glanced at the display, then stood. "I'm going to have to go outside and walk around. The storm system is interfering with the signal. Will you be okay here?"

"Of course. I'll clean up while you talk to Preston."

She watched him go, glad that he slipped through the outside door quickly. The Arctic breeze made her shudder and there was an air leak around the pet door that granted the badger's access.

Despite the roaring fire and the warmth of the stove, it was still in the low fifties inside the cabin. She missed her home and all her comforting rituals, like brewing a pot of her peppermint tea.

Determined not to get emotional, she finished clearing up, washing everything in a big basin of hot water, then went to stoke the fire. Minutes ticked by, and when Daniel failed to return, she went to the window and looked outside. He was standing in the clearing to the left of the house, still talking on his cell phone.

Seeing he was safe, she breathed a sigh of relief and went to sit by the fire.

Seconds later he came in and joined her. "Preston is sure we're dealing with someone with police training—or maybe a fireman. Have you had problems with anyone who fits that profile?"

"No, in fact the only people I know with that type of background work security at the natural gas plant."

"Are you friends or at least on friendly terms with any of them?"

"Besides you, there's Bruce, who's usually at the gate when I pass through, but that's it."

"I'll have someone speak to him," Daniel said.

"You haven't told me exactly why Preston thinks my stalker is in those professions."

"The absence of evidence all the way down the line," he said.

"This last time, the fire did the job for him."

"Maybe so, but trace evidence is nearly impossible to eradicate completely and that's what they're concentrating on now. The fire marshal and the police may find a clue at the doors and windows, depending on how he rigged those so we couldn't get out."

"We know one thing," she said, then seeing he was waiting for her to clarify, added, "He wants me dead by any means possible and is willing to take you along with me."

"I'm protecting you, so I'm a problem for him," Daniel said.

"There's no reason for both of us to stay in his line of fire."

"I'm not going anywhere, so don't bother bringing up that possibility with Martin. Like it or not, we're in this together. To him, I'm a loose end because he doesn't know how much you've told me."

"Why can't I reason this out?" she said, pacing. "I must have done something to get in this man's sights."

"Keep thinking about it until the answer comes to you," he said.

"All my life I've had to deal with the unexpected. As a kid I never knew what was going to happen next, so I was always going over possibilities, thinking about what-ifs. Talk about déjà vu. I've got to do the same thing now."

"After your mother passed away, things got really tough for you, didn't they?"

She nodded. "Whenever Dad was on a winning streak we always had plenty of everything, but that never lasted long. Sometimes there wasn't enough money to even buy food because he'd use all the cash we had to get back into a game. That's when I learned to fend for myself."

"How?"

"I started all kinds of little businesses—whatever I could do after school. I walked dogs, babysat, offered to wash people's cars or mow their lawns—whatever I could get that would earn me a few bucks," she said. "Dad had a gazillion enemies, but I had the ability to make friends at the drop of a hat. Maybe people just felt sorry for me back then."

"Did you ever feel sorry for yourself?"

"Sometimes, I guess, but I couldn't dwell on it. I had to be the strong one because I was the one without the addiction," she said. "I spent most of my time trying to make things better."

"You still do that. That might be part of the reason you love restoring old furniture."

She nodded. "I think TechTalk Inc. reflects some of that, too. I want to help people make the most from the world around them. That takes understanding new technologies so they can choose between the good and the bad."

"There are people who'll always object to change."

"If I were working to build a nuclear power plant in the Four Corners, I can see how I might make enemies who'd want me dead," she said. "The thing is, I'm just a spokesperson. I don't make decisions, I just explain what's being planned or is already in place."

"That's what has finally convinced me these attacks are personal. It's not what you do, it's who you are that's making him come after you."

"So we're back to where we started—nowhere." She took a deep breath, then let it out again. "Hiding out isn't going to solve the problem, though. Sooner or later I'll have to surface, and when I do, he's going to be there waiting for me."

THIRTY MINUTES LATER, they set out, having learned from Gene that the storm had produced only rain at the lower elevations. Holly checked the rearview mirror every few minutes even though the dirt road they were on only had one set of tracks in the snow—from Gene's pickup.

"Relax. He's not there," Daniel said quietly.

"He always comes at me out of nowhere," she whispered.

"I'm watching for him," he said, his jaw set. "Do you want to go directly to Martin's office?"

"No. I'd like to drive by my house first. Before I can go on, I need to face what's already happened. It'll be my way of finding closure, of making myself understand that although my things went up in smoke, I'm still here. He didn't destroy *me*."

"Your place is probably still a crime scene. If it hasn't been released yet, you won't be able to cross the yellow tape line. Why don't you call Preston and ask him what the status there is?" Daniel handed her his cell. "Press two."

Holly made the call, and when Bowman answered she pressed the button that put him on speaker. "Detective, I'd like to come in and take a look around my home," Holly said, surprised by how steady and calm she sounded. Inside, she was neither. "I'd like to know what, if anything, is left."

"It's still a crime scene, Ms. Gates," he said. "I've been

working with the arson investigator, and so far we know that the fire had multiple origins—the front and rear entrances, the roof in the rear and the east wall. The arsonist used an accelerant, probably white gas, one of the fuels used in camping stoves and lanterns."

"Four separate places.... He's really going all out now." Her voice shook but she cleared her throat to cover for it.

"Unfortunately for him, I'm very good at what I do. I'll catch him—guaranteed."

"Are you on-site now?" Daniel asked.

"Yeah—hang on," Preston said, then spoke to someone else.

Holly glanced at Daniel and felt a tug deep inside her. He'd made her battle his own. No one had ever stood by her like this. An ingrained caution warned her to fight her growing feelings for him, even as another part of her longed to surrender, to be swept away by the magic she'd found in his arms. Surrender... could it be so bad when it felt so right?

Bowman came back on the line. "The fire marshal found that the locking mechanism on the kitchen door was jammed from the outside with soft, lead wire. That's why it wouldn't open."

"I won't interfere with your investigation, but please let me come by and see what's there for myself," she said.

"All right, and while you're here I'd like you to look around and see if you can spot anything that doesn't belong. It's unlikely that this man left something behind that would lead us to him, but you never know."

As the call ended, Holly took a deep breath, fighting a deep-seated panic. "I've been attacked, chased, basically I'm homeless—"

"But you're still alive," he said, interrupting, "and we're going to keep you that way." He glanced over at her. "You've been through a lot, Holly, but it hasn't all been bad. You've made some great friends along the way—Gene, Preston, me and let's not forget Mr. Badger."

She smiled. "You're right. I won't focus on what's not right. It's what's working now that matters most."

The roads were clear once they reached lower elevations, as Gene had reported, so they made good time.

At her insistence, once they reached Hartley, Daniel stopped at a drive-through for some coffee. She wasn't desperate for the eye-opening brew, it was more of a delaying tactic. She wanted to make sure she'd be ready to face the scene at her house.

"You're scared," Daniel said as they waited in the car for their drinks, "but you don't need to be. The worst is over."

"It may not be," she said, then after sipping her coffee, continued, "The hardest thing about facing an enemy like this is I can't get away from him mentally."

"We all need to recharge from time to time. *Hosteen* Silver used to do that by going into his hogan," he said, driving down the highway again.

"And you and Gene?"

"Gene thrives on his ranch. It's back-breaking work, but he loves that place because it gives him a sense of continuity. Land is something that will always provide for you if you take care of it—those are his words, not mine."

"And you?"

He considered it before replying. "Everything I need is within me. It isn't based on where I am. My strength comes from knowing I've got the skills and instincts to handle myself no matter what comes my way."

"I envy you," she said softly.

She remained quiet as they drove into Hartley. She'd tried to prepare herself mentally as the miles had stretched past her window, yet the second her house came into view, her breath caught in her throat. What remained was a shell comprised of walls surrounded by scorched wood and rubble. The kitchen was recognizable only because of the blackened refrigerator that still stood in place, leaning slightly.

Daniel reached for her hand and she clung to it almost in desperation. She didn't want to be strong anymore. She wanted to throw herself into his arms, let his strength envelope her, and keep the hurt at bay.

He squeezed her hand and, with effort, she pushed back the darkness. "Okay, let's go take a look." Her words sounded brave, but inside all she felt was a hollowness that matched the empty shell her home had become.

Almost as if sensing that she needed him, he remained close by her as they walked toward the house.

As they approached, Holly saw three department vehicles parked along the curb and a crime scene van in the driveway. People, some uniformed officers and firemen, were gathered in clusters, or working alone inside the yellow tape line. A film crew from the local cable station was interviewing some official in a suit, and a fireman was taking photos.

Preston broke away from his work and walked up to meet them as they stepped onto the scorched yellow lawn, now damp from last night's rain. At least her yard would recover, she reminded herself, trying to find something positive to focus on.

"The places where the oak floor appears intact aren't necessarily safe to walk on. They've lost their support underneath, so watch your step," he warned. "Also be careful not to touch or lean on anything that may give way."

She nodded, staring at the house. Portions of the roof remained, although her porch and the area around the front door were completely destroyed.

"Where's the best access route?" Daniel asked.

"The fire department cut a hole through the west wall. Go through there. The floor around both exits is completely gone."

Holly swallowed hard, then followed Daniel. A gaping hole, crudely cut by a powerful saw judging from the piles of damp sawdust, led into the den. Grasping at anything she could to bolster her spirits, she took comfort in the fact that the room beyond seemed fairly intact. Maybe her photos had survived.

She pressed her purse to her side, reminding herself that no matter what, at least one memento remained untouched. She still had her mother's gift. Of all her possessions, nothing meant more to her than that.

As she picked her way through what was left of the rooms, she saw that what the flames hadn't destroyed smoke and water had. The shelves where her photos had been were now nothing more than blackened, charred wood soaked in water. "My photos…."

"Are still there inside you—images no one can ever take away," Daniel said.

His soft words seemed in sharp contrast to the stony look on his face. Yet she'd learned that was just his way. He never showed the world what was in his heart. His actions spoke for him and told her how much he cared.

They went down the hall and Holly discovered that her bedroom had sustained the least amount of damage. Although her bed and clothing were ruined, everything on the north wall remained untouched. Both her college diploma and her award certificate from the tribe in honor of her special services were intact.

"If only a few things were meant to survive, I'm glad these made it," she said, taking them off the wall and tucking them under one arm.

Minutes later, they stepped off the foundation and Preston came over to join them. "Anything?"

Holly shook her head. "What's in there…." Her voice suddenly broke despite her efforts, and she looked away.

"I better get back to work," Preston said. Giving her time to gather herself, he focused on Daniel. "Can I talk to you for a minute, bro?"

As they stepped away, Holly was glad for that moment alone. Seeing her home like this had been harder than she'd ever imagined. Yet it was time to move on. All her life she'd found

the strength to create something new from the ashes of what
could have been. She could do it again.

Though she'd been looking off into the distance, a prickle of
warmth spread through her. Obeying that instinctive knowing,
she turned and met Daniel's gaze.

In the midst of chaos he stood tall, offering strength. In his
eyes she saw honor and determination. Life would eventually place them along different paths. Yet, for now, he stood
between her and danger, an ally that would not be moved.

Leaving Preston by his squad car, Daniel joined her a
moment later as his brother drove away. "Are you okay?" he
asked.

She nodded. "I don't know if I've said this enough, or even
at all lately, but thanks…for everything."

"No thanks are needed," he said gruffly.

She knew instantly that she'd made him uncomfortable and
let it pass. "Once the guy after me watches the local news
tonight and sees all the people here, maybe he'll back off. He
won't need to keep coming after me just to prove what a bad
guy he is. He's already shown our entire community." Holly
raised her voice, trying to be heard over the roar of an accel-
erating motorcycle.

Before Daniel could answer, the motorcycle raced up onto
the sidewalk. As it bore down on them, the helmeted cyclist
raised his right arm and pointed a gun right at them.

Chapter Seventeen

Daniel tackled Holly to the ground as two shots rang out. One bullet whined past his ear like an angry bee, the second thumped into the ground so close the turf kicked up into his face.

Daniel rolled Holly in the opposite direction, hoping to throw off the man's next shot, but no third round came. Turning his head, he watched the motorcycle cut back into the street at the next driveway and roar off, leaving an acrid cloud of blue, oily smoke in its wake.

Daniel let go of Holly and jumped to his feet. "Stay down! I'm going after him."

Daniel pointed out Holly to an approaching officer as he raced for his SUV, cell phone in hand. Preston answered the call just as Daniel started the engine.

"A guy on a red dirt bike just breezed by and took a shot at us. He made a turn onto Tenth Street, going north," Daniel said. "I'm following in the SUV, but I don't have him in sight yet. Can you cut him off?"

"I'm on Twelfth, heading away, but maybe I can intercept him before he gets out of the neighborhood," Preston said. "What else did you get?"

"The shooter's packing a revolver. He's wearing blue coveralls, gloves and a black helmet with a tinted visor. The cycle makes a helluva racket, too, and smokes like a chimney," Daniel said. "I didn't get a make."

Daniel accelerated on the straightaway. The cloud of blue

smoke at the corner revealed the bike's path. "One more thing, Preston," he said. "The bike's tag was covered with something, maybe masking tape."

"Copy that. We've got two other units in the area, so we'll try to keep him from reaching the river."

Daniel knew the shooter, unlike them, could race up sidewalks and flood channels on that bike, and if he made it into the *bosque,* the wooded area on both sides of the river, he'd be gone for good.

Even as the thought formed, Daniel saw a cloud of blue smoke to his right. He took his foot off the gas and listened. The roar was to his left.

Turning the corner, he caught a glimpse of red as the cyclist darted past a black-and-white that had its emergency lights flashing. The roadblock was just a few seconds too late. The shooter was racing for the river, just as Preston had predicted.

Daniel shot past the squad car, closing on the cycle. If Preston reached the next intersection first, they'd trap the cycle between them.

Preston came back on the line. "I hear him coming, but I'm still a block east. Where are you, Dan?"

"Heading down Eleventh toward the park. He's got a hundred yards on me, but he's suddenly cut his speed."

The biker braked hard, fishtailing, then swerved left, passing between the vertical pipe barrier and raced down a ramp into the concrete-lined flood control ditch.

Daniel screeched to a stop, grabbed the phone and jumped out, running across the road. As he reached the barrier, all he could see was a thin veil of smoke and the rear end of the cycle. Four seconds later, the bike cut right, raced down a footpath into the *bosque* and disappeared into the riverside undergrowth.

"He made it to the *bosque* and headed down the foot trail," Daniel said, reporting in. "How many ways out of there, a dozen?"

"At least. Wish we had a chopper," Bowman said. "Is Holly okay?"

"She was when I left, and I signaled an officer to stay with her," Daniel said, jogging back toward the SUV.

It only took him a few minutes to get back to the burned-out house, and as he pulled up, Holly was sitting in a police cruiser. The officer beside it was watching the streets, but nodded when he pulled up. Parking behind the vehicle, Daniel walked up as she climbed out of the unit.

"You didn't catch him, did you?" she said, reading his expression.

When he saw the tears welling up in her eyes, he felt as if someone had punched him right in the gut. He'd never felt this kind of connection to anyone else in his life. "No, but there are others out there still looking for him," he said, wishing he had better news.

Holly shifted her gaze back to the house. "I really thought I'd prepared myself, but I guess I never let go of the hope that the fire damage would be less extensive."

"Our place is yours for as long as you want to stay there. My brothers and I will move whatever you need so you can have more room. If any of your own furnishings can be salvaged, we'll be happy to take them there for you, too. It may make the cabin feel more like home," he said, leading her away.

As she smiled, a tear fell down her cheek, but she wiped it quickly away. "Does Mr. Badger get a vote?"

"Nah, he's strictly a silent partner."

AFTER GIVING STATEMENTS to the sergeant at the scene, they set out once again.

"I haven't called Martin and rescheduled," she said.

"Don't. No one needs to know your plans in advance," Daniel said. "He'll understand, and if not, I'll *explain* it to him." His tone clearly gave the word another meaning, and to his relief, she laughed. He couldn't stand seeing her cry.

"I'm not sure Martin's going to want me to continue being the plant's spokesperson at job fairs and PR gatherings anymore, at least not until this lunatic is caught."

"It won't be long before he's behind bars. He's getting reckless and taking too many chances," Daniel said.

"I'm letting this get to me again. I'm sorry. Seeing my home like that was harder than I thought. It was going to be mine forever, or that's what I thought when I moved in."

"Forever... I know that's important to you, but there's no forever, not really."

"It depends on how you define it. To me, forever is something that'll last as long as I do. Secure tomorrows, that's what I've spent my adult life working for, and what my *casita* represented," she said, then continued in a stronger voice, "I'll rebuild it, of course, but it's going to be a new dream now...."

Her sadness tore into him. Unsure of what to say, Daniel stared straight ahead. Maybe this was a wake-up call for him, too. What the hell was he doing thinking seriously about a woman who saw permanence and stability as her primary goals? Yet there was something about Holly that brought out a side of him he'd never known existed—and one he liked. Around her he felt like the hero who could defeat any odds, a man who was needed, in every sense.

He was losing his mind. It was that simple. Her aching vulnerability and quiet courage sucked him in, making him want to do whatever was necessary to keep her safe—and more important, by his side. He wanted Holly in every way a man could want a woman, and maybe that was part of the problem. If they could have one night of crazy, steamy sex then that pull might dwindle to nothing—but, if not, then what?

"What are you thinking?" she asked.

"After I left *Hosteen* Silver's, I found that I didn't want a home base anymore. It only tied me down," he said, ducking the question. "My warehouse office-home was only a temporary stop on the road to bigger dreams. Proving I could make a place for myself anywhere was important to me. I wanted to enjoy the same freedom as the hawk who nests in Copper Canyon."

"Yes, but even the hawk has its nest," she said.

And a mate, he realized silently.

"*Hosteen* Silver told me once that like the hawk, I needed to learn the gift of stillness, that only then would I be able to see what was important and what wasn't. Back then I had no idea what he was talking about, but I'm beginning to see that movement isn't necessarily freedom. I'm going to have to rethink some things." Like what he'd do when it was time to say goodbye to this woman—who had the power to turn all his ideas upside down. She'd leave a gaping hole right through the middle of his heart.

They arrived at the natural gas plant twenty minutes later. He saw her tug at her slacks and try to smooth them out.

"I should have bought some new clothes," she said.

"You look fine," he said, then seeing her look of disbelief, added, "really."

She took a deep breath. "I may have to sell myself to Martin all over again. I need to remind him that I do good work, and that he needs me."

"Be careful about volunteering information. Remember that for all we know, Martin's our enemy. He has the right build, and the physical fitness to do the job. He also knows your address, schedule and what hours you keep. Don't let your guard down around him."

She nodded somberly. "I hate this—having to look at people I know through jaded eyes and not trusting anyone. That's just not me."

"Survival is at the heart of all of us. Think of it in those terms, and you'll find it's a much better fit."

THOUGH SHE HADN'T GIVEN Martin advance notice, he seemed glad to see them. He stood when they appeared at his office door, and waved them toward chairs.

"A friend of mine in the Hartley Police Department called to tell me about the shooting incident," Martin said, moving back behind his desk. "Please fill me in on the details."

Holly and Daniel sat down, but Martin remained on his feet. He paced as they spoke, stopping occasionally by the window and glancing outside.

"From the beginning of all this I should have recommended that you take a leave of absence, Holly," Martin said, turning to face her at last. "The problem is that we needed to keep the momentum of this project going—and we still do."

"I understand. What we have to do is work around what's happening."

"You're his target, that's clear enough. So let's get you off this guy's turf for a while." Martin stopped pacing and faced them. "We can do that by temporarily redefining your duties."

"Whatever you need," she said and waited.

Martin brought out a topographic map and handed it to her. "Judging from the public's response, the biggest challenge we're facing is proving to locals that the water table won't be compromised. We're already taking water samples from area wells to test, but we're also going to need water samples from the river leading into our power plant. That'll give us a quality level to compare with the wastewater we'll be releasing, and future output from those same water wells."

She nodded. "No change in water quality means no contamination. So exactly what is it that you're asking me to do?" she asked.

"Your file says your degree is in ecology," Martin said. "You've done field work, correct?"

Holly nodded. "During my senior year, I spent three months working for the Rio Grande Conservancy District."

"So why did you turn to PR work?" Daniel asked.

"A degree in ecology and $3.50 would buy me a cup of coffee. It's not a good career degree unless you plan to teach,"

Holly said. "But my science background is perfect for what I do now."

"You can put those college courses to good use in another way this time," Martin said. "I'd like you to go collect water samples from the high country where the water originates as snow pack, then enters the river's tributaries. If you're up to it."

"Of course I am. However, to go into the middle of nowhere when someone's after me... I don't know," she said slowly.

"It might actually be the best strategy," Daniel said. "There'll be plenty of cover while we're in the forest, plus it'll be a break from your routine. That'll make it harder for your enemy to track you," Daniel said, then glanced at Martin. "You'll keep this assignment under wraps, correct?"

"Absolutely. We want to get our samples without anyone interfering, or worse, contaminating the process."

"From a security standpoint, getting away *is* a sound idea," Daniel said looking at Holly.

"I've gone camping before, but all my stuff went up in smoke," she said. "Since it's winter, we would need to get heavy-duty outdoor clothing, and special gear, too."

"The tribe will provide you with whatever's necessary, including freeze-dried food," Martin said, then looked at Daniel. "Security has extreme weather equipment on hand for training ops. Take whatever you need. If there's something you don't find there, purchase it retail and put it on the expense account."

As they left Martin's office and headed down the hall to the security offices, Holly remained silent.

"What's bothering you?" Daniel asked.

"I don't see Martin as a suspect, but if you really believe he could be behind this, then he'll know where we are," she whispered. "Won't that turn us into easy targets, and make us even more vulnerable? It would take a long time for any help to arrive where we're going."

"He'll know our general location, but trying to pinpoint

anyone in that forested section of the reservation will be nearly impossible," Daniel said. "The only person who'll have access to our GPS signal is Gene. He'll back us up if necessary."

"How can you be so sure Gene will do it? You haven't even asked him yet."

"I don't have to ask him to know the answer. We're brothers. We all help each other."

"You've got a really close, loving family."

"Yeah, I suppose," he said, suddenly uncomfortable. Women—why did they always have to *talk* about feelings? Actions—that's what mattered.

They arrived at the security equipment storeroom and went straight to the lockers where the outdoor gear was stored. "We hold training exercises during bad weather all the time, so we should find everything we need here."

"I sure wish I still had my own gear," she said. "I had a great backpack and the perfect down sleeping bag."

"We've got Arctic survival mummy bags that are as light as those feathers. Once we find a backpack frame that fits your body, all it'll take is a little adjustment. We have Gore-Tex jackets, too, like those used on Everest expeditions. I guarantee you'll be warm and dry."

"Great, but what about hiking boots? I wear size five and a half."

Daniel pointed to a large closet area. "We have women security officers your size. Take a look around and get whatever you need. There are wool socks in there, too—and don't worry, we don't recycle those. They're all new."

Ten minutes later, they loaded their gear and supplies into Daniel's vehicle. "We'll go past Copper Canyon up to the trailhead," he announced.

Holly nodded. "Sounds good to me."

TWO HOURS LATER, they were on the narrow footpath leading up a mountainside. Everything was going according to plan.

"I'm glad for this chance to get away," Holly said, turning her head to look at him. Daniel had insisted on covering her back. It wasn't likely anyone was ahead of them now.

Daniel picked his way across a rocky section in the trail where a misstep could easily result in a broken leg. "I like being outdoors, too. The only rules I've got to follow here are Mother Nature's."

"It always looks so peaceful in these piñon juniper woodlands, but there's a lot going on beneath the surface. Animals wage a daily battle for their own survival."

"Life *is* a struggle. Although the front lines differ for everyone, it requires heart to keep going," Daniel said.

"Or stubborness," she said with a smile as she stopped to catch her breath. "The man after me is persistent, but I'll outlast him. I dislike confrontations, but I won't give up, and that's why he won't win."

"I'll be right there to make sure he doesn't, too. I…care… about you," he said.

Her breath caught in her throat, and for a heartbeat, she didn't even move, afraid to spoil the moment. "You do?"

"How could you *not* know that?" he asked gruffly.

"You've never said so."

"I didn't think I had to." He glanced away from her and looked upward, instantly shifting the focus of their conversation. "Clouds are creeping in and the wind's picking up. Look at those ponderosa pines on that high ridge. Is that snow? We should have paid more attention to the weather forecast."

She sighed. So much for the moment. Daniel wasn't big on tender words, but there was something wonderful about actually having heard Daniel tell her that she was special to him. Holly knew that their time together would be short. Soon they'd go their separate ways and that's why moments mattered so much. Those sweet words would wrap themselves around her heart and become a memory she'd always treasure.

Holly zipped up her jacket and adjusted her wool cap. "I

thought the cold front was still in California and we'd have another thirty-six hours before the storm reached New Mexico."

"Forecasters aren't always on target and local conditions fluctuate. We're going to be getting the leading edge before long. I can feel the moisture."

They hiked for another hour, hunkering down against the increasingly cold breeze as they climbed across a rocky, barren knoll. As they drew closer to the area where they'd be taking their first water sample, a meadow surrounded by thickets of spruce, fir and aspens, the wind suddenly picked up. Leaves, pines needles and small branches blew everywhere. Lightning lit up the darkened sky followed by a boom so loud it shook the ground. Holly jumped, then reached for him.

"I'm here," he said, holding her close.

"Can you smell the ozone?" she said, burying herself in his arms. "That was so close I could actually hear the crackle before the boom."

She *hated* lightning storms. She'd had to face too many of them alone, always at night, wondering when her dad would return home from a card game.

As the conifers up ahead rustled, waves of freezing sleet descended. The drops were so cold they stung her face.

Daniel pulled her into a rocky overhang that provided partial shelter. "We can't go much farther. We've got to get out of this storm and make camp before it gets dark."

"We also need to get off this ridge fast, particularly now that there's lightning," she said.

Daniel slipped the backpack off his shoulders and pulled out a forest service map he'd kept in a zippered pocket, preferring it to the GPS display.

As she reached inside her own backpack for a flashlight, a six-inch brown teddy bear popped up along with it. It was almost as if it had come out to take a look around for himself, and it made her smile. Somehow seeing the old, tattered toy renewed her courage.

"That fur ball thing might need a raincoat if it stays out any longer," Daniel said.

"It's a teddy bear, not a thing," she said, laughing, then shined the flashlight on the map so he could get a clearer look.

"We're about here," he said, pointing. "There's supposed to be a cave up ahead, just off the trail."

"That would protect us from the storm, but there's no telling what else lives in there."

"We'll check it out first. It'll be okay," he said, his voice low, his gaze steady.

His words caressed and comforted her, awakening feelings that were even more dangerous than the storm. He was a man of few words, and maybe that was why whatever he said carried such an impact.

As a fierce gust of wind slammed against their faces, he looked uphill. "Let's go find that cave." He squeezed her hand gently. "We can watch nature put on her show from there."

She bit back a sigh. Nature's most powerful forces wouldn't be outside, raging in the wind, hail and snow. It would be in the stillness of a look, or a tender touch in the silence.

Chapter Eighteen

As they entered the shallow cave, Daniel surveyed it in a glance. The place was really nothing more than a domed recess—a mini amphitheater in the cliffside about twenty-feet high at the peak and extending about fifteen feet into the mountain.

"It's not much of a cave, but at least we're out of the wind and sleet," he said, taking off his soaked backpack and placing it against one of the dry, sloping sides of the sandstone cavern.

"I'm just glad we've got shelter," Holly said, setting her backpack down and studying the natural enclosure.

"What do you say we place the tent on that high spot in the back? In here we won't have to stake it down, but it'll keep the wind that's coming through the opening off us. Once we get that done, we can bring out our stove. Hot coffee would really hit the spot right now."

The light nylon tent took less than five minutes to set up. Next they unfolded the metal stove, and soon afterward, they had hot water for instant coffee.

"How about dinner?" he asked her. "We don't need to heat the MREs. If you mix the packet up, it warms itself inside the bag."

"I've had them before," she said, "but I'm not hungry right now. I bought some peanut butter cookies from the vending machine at the plant. That and the coffee will do me just fine."

Seated on top of a foam sleeping pad, they sipped their coffee. "Sleet's still coming down in waves, but despite that, if the thunder would just go away, it wouldn't seem so bad," Holly said.

"You've got peanut butter cookies—and me. What more could you ask for?" Daniel said.

She laughed.

"See that? Things aren't so bad."

Daniel placed his arm around her shoulders, and she leaned into him. She loved his scent. A mixture of the rugged outdoors—sage and piñon and a trace of spicy aftershave. As she lay nestled against him, she could hear the steady drumming of his heart. More than anything she wished she could have stayed there forever.

Daniel tightened his hold. "We're warm and together. Let that be enough for now."

The anxious moments of the past few days drifted out of her thoughts as gentler, yet stronger emotions spread through her.

She was falling in love, everything feminine in her knew it, but it made no sense. How could two people who were so wrong for each other be so perfect together?

"I like the way you feel against me," he said gruffly.

She snuggled deeper into him as the lightning continued to light up the skies outside and the ground shook. No matter what forces raged around her, she knew nothing would harm her as long as he was by her side. "I've always hated winter thunderstorms. Snow is supposed to be quiet—peaceful."

"You make too many rules. Give yourself more freedom and see what happens."

Daniel angled his head and took her lips gently. "Listen only to me—and feel," he whispered, his breath hot on her mouth.

He kissed her again, his tenderness persuading without insisting. She parted her lips, drinking in the taste of him. The desire to surrender control, to let him lead her into a world of fire and need thrummed through her.

As she melted into him, he groaned. "You're all heat and softness."

She drew in a shaky breath. "I feel like I'm tumbling out of control."

"Don't tumble, slide gently into my arms.…"

He took her hand and eased it inside his shirt, pressing it against his skin.

As she gazed into Daniel's eyes, she saw the raw passion there and it took her breath away. She could still back away, but she knew she'd spend the rest of her life wondering and regretting what might have been.

"It's just you and me. Do we need anything else?" he asked.

"Show me what's in your heart," she whispered. "I don't want to wonder anymore."

He drew in a breath, then lowered his mouth to hers. His kiss was possessive, yet achingly tender. She sighed as he drew back just enough to leave a trail of moist kisses down the column of her neck.

"Feel the fire," he said, pushing her sweater and bra out of his way and tasting the tips of her breasts.

She'd been cold with only coffee to warm her. Now a searing heat filled her, followed by longings too intense to deny.

Daniel picked her up, then carried her out of the cold and into the tent. As he set her down, the storm she saw in his eyes made the power of the lightning outside pale in comparison.

He tugged at her clothes, branding the skin he bared with his mouth until she cried out. She invited everything, and when she could give nothing more, he moved away.

Daniel unbuckled his belt with one hand, and stripped off his clothes. As she watched him, a new need stirred inside her. She wanted to touch him, to memorize every facet of Daniel.

When he returned to her, she shifted, and gently pushed him back so he lay beneath her. Holding his gaze, she straddled him and kissed the muscular ripples on his chest.

She learned quickly what gave him pleasure, and the fire

that gripped them intensified. As lightning screamed through the skies, his control snapped. He gripped her hips hard, brought her down against him and entered her.

Holly surrendered to the fire, needing him, wanting everything with a greed that matched his own. As the storm roared, Holly felt herself shatter, shudders rocking her soul.

He followed her over that brittle edge, then held her tightly as she collapsed over him, too exhausted to move.

"You make me feel whole," he whispered, his arms wrapped tightly around her.

Time passed, but she never moved away. Slowly she felt him grow hard again. "No one's ever made me feel the way you do," she said. "Beautiful, feminine, needed."

She heard his throaty growl then the fire gripped them once again.

DAYBREAK CREPT inside the cave, but the temperature remained icy. As she opened her eyes, she realized that she was alone in the sleeping bag. Outside the tent, just beyond her view, she could hear Daniel moving around. She dressed quickly and went to meet him.

"Good morning," he said, as she came out. "About time you got up. It's clear outside and the ground is warming up. We can get those water samples and head back before the next wave of the storm hits—if one's still coming."

She saw that he'd already stowed away most of their supplies. She wasn't sure what she'd expected from him this morning, but the abrupt return to reality jolted her and left her feeling vaguely disappointed.

"Regrets?" he asked, accurately reading her expression.

"No," she answered, *not in the way you mean.* Yet even as she spoke, she could feel a coldness growing inside her. As she struggled to hold on to what they'd discovered in each other's arms, its reality seemed to slip through her fingers, dissolving away.

Sunlight, strong and clear, streamed through the opening in the cave as the sun rose in the east. In the dark of night the differences between them hadn't mattered. Now, in the light of day, everything seemed different—and maybe it was. What they'd shared had been rooted in hopes and wishes. They'd tried to make the impossible real, and had been blinded by the fire they'd found in each other's arms.

A bone-deep sadness filled her as they ate a mostly silent breakfast of MRE bacon and scrambled eggs, sipping instant coffee in metal cups.

"Do you think he'll still be out there when we get back to Hartley?" she asked.

"Yes, and I'd be willing to bet he's been going nuts searching for you," he said. "Once we return, it won't take him long to pick up our trail. He's good. That's why I'm thinking we shouldn't hurry back. We have enough food and water to stay a few more days, and that'll give Preston and the other officers more time to work the case."

She thought of spending more nights with Daniel, and the possibility was tempting. Yet, deep inside, she knew it would be a mistake. She wanted a committed relationship—permanence—the kind of love that couldn't be taken from her. Yet loving a man like Daniel wasn't about holding on tightly. It was about letting the winds of freedom dance between them.

"Ready?" Daniel asked, interrupting her thoughts.

With the tent stowed away and their backpacks on, they stepped to the mouth of the cave. Everything outside was covered in a wisping fog, and with the bright sunlight coming from above, the forest shimmered gently. It was as if nature itself was basking in the glow of the magic Daniel and she had found in each other's arms.

"Let's go," Daniel said bringing her focus back, "but stay alert."

"You think he may have tracked us here?" she asked quickly.

"He's surprised us before, but don't worry too much about it now. We'll meet the problem if it comes."

As THEY SET OUT Daniel saw the shadow of fear return to her eyes. He wished that he could have replaced it with the utter contentment he'd seen on her face as she'd lain asleep on his chest early this morning.

Although he'd hoped that once they'd made love he'd get her out of his system, he'd found the opposite was true. Daniel shifted his pack and stepped onto the trail, feeling the weight of the handgun strapped to his belt and the hunting knife in its sheath against his leg.

The weather had cleared and their stalker had undoubtedly expanded his search, so there could be no more distractions. Emotions clouded a man's outlook and he was in a life-or-death fight against an enemy who didn't give up. He had to push all personal feelings aside now and focus solely on the job. He'd grown to know his enemy, and instinct and experience told him that they'd come face-to-face soon.

Daniel had to slow his pace, finding the trail either muddy or slippery from leftover moisture, especially in the low spots. "Three miles ahead is a meadow, then above that, the snow-melt fed lake."

"That's where I need to take the first sample," she said.

He turned back and looked over the low ridge to the east. This trail was familiar to him. Somewhere down below was the head of Copper Canyon.

Holly was walking at an easy pace, and as he watched her hips swaying gracefully, he thought once again of last night and smiled. She'd come alive in his arms, and for those moments, she'd forgotten everything except the passion in her heart.

A shower of small rocks suddenly exploded from the wall of the cliff just above Holly, and a second later a loud crack sounded, traveling up the pass from behind and below. He reacted in an instant, shoving Holly down just as another rifle shot echoed up the mountain.

"Hug the ground," he said, reaching for his pistol. "Stay out of his line of sight."

Her eyes were wide as she lay on her side, staring back down the trail. "*How* did he find us?"

"Worry about that later. Based on the timing between the bullet strike and the sound, he's still several hundred yards away. That rifle gives him a definite advantage, so we've got to keep him as far away from us as possible. We're going to have to move fast so lose your gear."

She nodded, slipping her pack off.

"Take only what's absolutely necessary—water, matches, cell phone, GPS and your canteen," Daniel said, slipping out of his own pack while keeping an eye on the trail.

Thinking quickly, he grabbed two energy bars from the zippered pouch, then looked back down the trail. "The fog's shifting again. He can't see us now, but it won't be long before it dissipates and we'll be clear targets. Hurry."

"All set," Holly said a second later.

As he turned to look, she shoved the stuffed bear into her jacket, then zipped it back up again.

"What?" she asked, seeing the bemused look on his face. "I said I'm ready to go."

"Hike up the trail until we get out of this pass, then turn south and move into the tree line. I'll guard your back."

"So much for collecting water samples," she said, rising to a crouch.

"Next time." He glanced back, thinking of their enemy, just out of his reach. Someday soon that would change.

Chapter Nineteen

An hour later, they were descending a steep incline, half stumbling, half sliding through a grove of tall, old pines. They'd gone downhill, angling back in the direction of the trailhead, but were forced to stay behind cover each step of the way. Out in the open, even at a quarter mile, Daniel knew they could be picked off with a rifle.

"He's got to know we're heading back toward your SUV—assuming he knows where we parked," Holly said, her voice coming in gasps.

She was fit, but this was a forced march and she was used to pacing herself at this altitude. Daniel, several feet behind her and uphill, stopped, giving her a chance to breathe, and looked down.

"I've got an idea that may slow him just a little," Daniel said. "He'll be following our tracks closely and, undoubtedly, hopes to catch up before we reach a road. He'll be looking ahead, far more worried about an ambush, and might not be watching where he puts his feet. Let's use that to our advantage and set up a trap."

"You've got my vote," she said, walking up to him and looking at a fallen log. "What do you have in mind?"

SEVERAL MINUTES LATER, they were on the move again, going parallel along the ridge below the tree line instead of descending into the narrow canyon below. They were side by side now, with Daniel to her right, uphill a few yards from her.

"I hope he breaks his neck. That log is a good obstacle. He'll have to go over or around it, and either way he's going to find trouble," Holly said.

"It'll roll like a ball the second he puts a foot on it. If he steps over it instead, there's that nice hole we left for him under those leaves. An injury, even a slight one, will get him off our backs for a while," Daniel said. "You up for a climb?" He cocked his head to the right.

"I think you have a second guardian animal—the mountain goat," she grumbled. "Are you thinking of circling back up and hitting the trail?"

"Exactly. We can make really good time that way. If we keep following this route we'll have to go crashing through the trees and ground cover, and that'll make way too much noise." He grabbed her hand and pulled her up beside him. "Go ahead and take point. I'll be right behind you."

Twenty minutes later, after a hard climb, they reached the trail again, this time about a mile down from where they'd spent the night in the cave. Daniel studied the ground and cursed. "He's either smart, lazy or both. He came up as far as the cave, saw where we'd left the trail and headed back. Those tracks are fresh," he said.

"He knows where we're going, obviously back to the SUV, so he's waiting for us somewhere ahead—in ambush," she said.

"We need to figure out where he's hiding and make sure we don't turn ourselves into easy targets."

"Hopefully we'll be able to get a cell phone signal farther down the mountain," she said. "Then we can call for help."

"Maybe so, but for right now, I'm going to take the lead. You're the target, and I'm the one with the gun." Without waiting for a response, Daniel started down the trail.

Several hours later, they were within a half mile of the SUV. The sun was low in the sky, and it was difficult looking to the west even with sunglasses and a billed cap.

"This is a very bad tactical situation," Daniel whispered.

"Once we top that next saddle, the trail leads straight down the slope to the SUV. He's undoubtedly there somewhere, in position to physically cut us off, even if he misses us with the rifle. The sun's in our eyes, so he has the advantage."

Holly gave him a shaky smile, then looked south down the ridge. "We could work our way to the valley that way under cover, but there's still the meadow at the bottom. There are a few tall shrubs and some brush, but it's pretty open. The only other options I can see for us is to wait till dark."

"Even if it's pitch-black, he'll still be able to hear us crossing that section of loose gravel. There's also that ledge about fifty feet from the bottom that we'd have to navigate," he said. "We have to find an alternate route. Staying on this trail is nothing short of suicide."

"What area is he least likely to be watching?" she asked.

"North," he said after a beat. "To check that direction, he'd have to turn around and take his eye off our most likely route. But there's a downside, too. If he spots us crossing that rock face, we'll be caught out in the open and it's a good hundred yards of exposure."

Holly brought out the cell phone. "Let's try one more time to get a signal, then decide."

TEN MINUTES LATER, they were off the trail, circling around to their right, heading up toward the open ridge to the north. No call had been possible, but Daniel had composed a text message to Gene explaining the situation. All it would take is a silent touch to send once they had a signal.

No talking was possible now. They had to be extremely careful. The slightest mistake could put them in the crosshairs.

Once in position, just out of sight of the SUV, which was a quarter of a mile away, they remained in a crouch and waited, watching for any sign of their assailant. Time passed slowly, each minute stretching out into an eternity.

At long last Daniel spotted movement, then pointed out

the figure of a man in camouflage green and browns behind cover at the foot of the ridge. He had a rifle in his hands and was turning his head back and forth, watching the trail and the meadow to the south.

Daniel gestured for Holly to follow him. Although the range was ridiculously long for a handgun, he'd be able to force their enemy to stay low, and give him something to worry about.

Daniel made his way down carefully. More than once he felt a boulder rock under his weight, throwing him slightly off balance. A fall could easily be fatal here, if not from the rocks, then from the oncoming bullets.

As he glanced back at Holly, she looked up at him instead of at the path, and slipped. She recovered instantly, but not before a trickle of rocks went bounding downhill.

A barrage of gunfire followed and Holly dove behind a boulder, Daniel seconds behind her. One bullet ricocheted off the rock with a high-pitched whine.

"Help me push this," Daniel said, putting his shoulder to the large rock.

"That's our cover! Are you crazy?"

"Do it. Once it starts to tumble, hug the ground," he said.

The boulder finally gave under the combined pressure, rolled a few feet, then crashed into other rocks with a loud clack. Those rocks then tumbled down, striking others, and the momentum continued. Within a few seconds, hundreds of rocks were sliding, tumbling or falling down the talus slope.

The shooter snapped off a few quick shots before having to make a run for it.

"Move now before he starts shooting again," Daniel said.

They raced into the underbrush, their noise covered by the ominous rumble of the rockslide. Soon they reached a hiding spot about fifty yards west of the SUV.

Looking out from the thick cover, they saw that two of the tires were flat. From their hiding spot in an arroyo they could also see the gunman standing beside a black four-wheel drive SUV.

"We'll have to forget about my SUV. Even if the tires weren't flat, there's no way we'd reach it in one piece," Daniel whispered. "Keep going down the arroyo. Once we make it to the road, we should be within cell phone range."

"It won't take him long to realize where we're going when we don't show up here. My guess is that he'll start cruising up and down the road, waiting for us to poke our heads out."

He nodded. "I know. That's why we're going north again, over to Copper Canyon and the house we built with *Hosteen Silver*—what we all called home."

"Do you think this guy knows where it is?" she asked.

"Maybe. I don't have any way of gauging how much he's learned about me and my history, but he's proven to be very good at gathering intelligence."

"How did he find us? I can't figure it out. Nobody except Martin and Gene knew where we were going," she said.

"We'll have to deal with those questions when we get back. Right now, we need to focus on getting away. Stay sharp," he said.

An hour later, they descended the trail above Copper Canyon. As they hurried toward a stucco frame house several hundred yards farther down and across a meadow, Daniel spoke to Gene on the cell phone and explained their situation.

Daniel shoved the cell phone back into his pocket just as they heard a vehicle coming up the trail to their right. "Cut through those trees and head for the front door," he said, spotting the black SUV.

As they raced directly toward the house, the SUV was forced to circle around a deep wash. Daniel groped in his pocket as he ran, reaching for the house key. "There's no bridge over the arroyo, so he'll have to circle around. We'll reach the house ahead of him," he told Holly.

Daniel sprinted toward the porch, unlocked the dead bolt

and flung open the door. Holly ran inside and he closed the door behind him, locking up again.

"You plan to make a stand here until help can arrive?" Holly asked, swallowing hard as she looked around the room, which was sparsely furnished with wood-framed furniture.

"We're not staying, but I'm going to need you to start a fire in the fireplace. There are matches on the hearth, a stack of old newspapers and kindling right beside it," Daniel said, looking outside between the gap of one of the shuttered windows. "We've got three minutes, give or take."

"We're not staying, but you want me to build a fire? Are you that cold?" she said, working quickly.

He took one of the chairs from around the kitchen table and wedged it against the doorknob. "It's for show."

"I don't get it," she said, lighting the fire.

"You will." Daniel grabbed her hand. "Let's go."

They ran out of the back door moments later, locking it behind them, then headed down a narrow trail leading into the woods.

"Now I get it," Holly said after a moment. "The lights are on but nobody's home."

Smoothing away the few tracks they'd left, Daniel then led her farther into the trees. As they reached the heavy brush, they heard a vehicle pulling up in front of the house.

"Keep going," Daniel urged.

They ran for another hundred yards, then dropped down into an arroyo. The ground was damp, but sandy, not sticky. Staying below ground level, they remained hidden by the scant scrub brush that bordered the ditch. Moving quickly they made their way toward the highway.

"Once we reach the road, we'll need to get a ride fast—like from the first car that comes along," Daniel said. "I'm going to flag them down."

She looked at Daniel, her gaze taking him in quickly, and shook her head. "Any smart driver will steer around you and keep on going. You're armed, but you don't have a badge to show. You're just plain scary looking right now with that gun at your waist."

He gave her a confused look.

"Trust me. I'll handle this part."

Five minutes later, they reached the highway via the arroyo, then climbed up to road level. Seeing a pickup coming in their direction, she looked over at Daniel. "Hide your pistol, stay back and let me handle this."

She slipped off her heavy jacket, letting it fall to the ground as she stepped out onto the pavement. In a move that took her less than ten seconds, she unfastened her bra and pulled it out through her sleeve.

Holly stepped out into the lane, then waved the hot-pink, lacy, designer garment in the air. A few seconds later, the pickup, with at least two passengers, came to a screeching stop.

"Hi, boys!" Holly called out. "Got room for me and a friend?"

Chapter Twenty

As the passenger side door was thrown open, Holly smiled at the men. "Thanks, guys."

Daniel approached, holding Holly's jacket, and studied the men at a glance. Their dusty coveralls, and sweat stained caps with a local drilling company's logo, identified them as roughnecks riding home after pulling an all-nighter.

"You can ride in the cab with us, sweetheart," the younger one said, then gave Daniel a guarded look. "Dude, it's pretty crowded. You're going to have to ride in the back."

Daniel met his gaze and held it with a steely-eyed look that made the guy look away. "She can sit by the window," the man added quickly.

"Just behave, boys," Daniel said, his voice a low growl.

Moments later they were on their way to Hartley. It was colder than ice riding in the bed of the truck, but gritting his teeth, Daniel crouched low near the cab, out of the air stream, and used the time to call and update Gene.

"She did *what?*" Gene said, then burst out laughing.

"Yeah, you heard me," he grumbled into the phone. "I need you to pick us up. How about we meet at the Terminal Café on East Main next to the truck stop? I'll ask our ride to drop us off."

"You've got it. In the meantime, I'll see if I can find out how you were tracked."

"Go to Roanhorse first. The trail starts there," Daniel said.

It took another hour of freezing cold before they reached

town. As they were dropped off by the popular coffee shop, Daniel saw Gene exiting his own extended cab pickup.

Daniel turned to Holly, who was looking toward the café. "Help has arrived," he said, pointing ahead.

Seeing Gene, Holly waved. "Good. Now we can all go inside and you can warm up. You were probably freezing, riding in that open bed."

"I managed."

They were sitting in a booth moments later. With a steaming cup of coffee before him, Daniel turned to his left and glared at Holly, seated beside him. "Don't *ever* pull something like that bra stunt again."

"We didn't exactly have a lot of options. As you very clearly pointed out, we had to get a ride *fast,* and that meant the first set of wheels we saw. Mission accomplished." She paused. "But I am sorry you had to freeze all the way into town."

He grunted, then took a long swallow of coffee. "What did you get from Martin?" Daniel asked, looking across the table at Gene.

"He was surprised as hell, and told me that the only way someone could have accessed that information was if they'd hacked into the tribal system, then into his own files."

"Who else has his password?" Daniel asked.

"According to Martin, just his assistant, Joe Yazzie. But Yazzie wasn't in the office when Martin and I spoke."

"Take us to the plant," Holly said. "I want to talk to Martin face-to-face. If he's lying or covering up something, I'll know."

Both men exchanged worried glances.

"Guys, I've worked with Martin for the past two years on various projects. I *know* how to read him. When he's uneasy, he has a way of tugging at his earlobe or playing with his pen. If I ask him straight-out if he shared our whereabouts with anyone, and he starts doing, either, we'll know he's involved."

Daniel nodded. "Okay, then. We go there next."

"What about your SUV? You want me to take care of that for you?" Gene asked. "You said two of the tires were flat."

"Yeah, hopefully that's all he did to it, but you should call the tribal police and fill them in first. The tires and the vehicle itself are evidence, and they may want to check them out before they release it back to you."

Gene nodded. "Why don't you take my truck for now? *Hosteen* Silver's pickup is back at your office, and I can use it for transportation while I'm here."

"You sure about this? That truck's your baby. I can rent something," Daniel said.

"Yeah, you could, but not with an engine like mine. This truck's built for off-road work. It'll go anywhere a Jeep can, and has a lot better highway performance."

"All right, then. I can use the extra power."

"Just remember one thing, bro," Gene said. "If you get it all shot up, you bought it. I depend on those wheels to haul hay out to my cattle and horses when I'm hip-deep in snow."

"You've got yourself a deal—and thanks," Daniel said. "Since we're going to take your truck, let's head to my office instead. We can exchange rides there and not leave you without transportation."

"I could use some time to wash up, too," Holly said, glancing down at herself. "I smell like campfire smoke, and...dirt."

"I always liked that outdoorsy scent myself," Gene said, nudging her playfully with his elbow as they walked back to his pickup.

Daniel yanked Gene aside, taking his place beside Holly. "Hands off. Don't make me have to get rough with you."

Gene laughed. "You've been out in the cold too long, city boy? You're way too soft to take me on."

"Keep dreaming."

As they climbed into Gene's truck and pulled out, Holly began looking behind them. "How long do you think it'll be before he finds us again?"

"Doesn't matter. There are three of us in the fight right now, and I don't think he's going to risk those odds," Gene said, then glanced at Daniel.

"I agree with that," Daniel said. "I've noticed that he's changed his tactics. He's become more patient—a planner. He won't strike again until he thinks he's got a clear advantage."

"Do you think you may be dealing with a dirty cop? That would explain the lack of evidence at the scenes, his fighting skills and maybe even the way he gathers intel on you," Gene said.

"That really does fit," Holly said slowly. "A law enforcement officer would have access to many databases and be able to get cooperation from most people and agencies. The only problem with that is I don't know any police officers except for Preston."

"It's still an interesting theory. Let's not discard it altogether, at least not until we get more to go on," Daniel said.

They arrived at Daniel's office a short time later. As they got out of the truck, Gene tossed his brother the key.

"Do you want me to stick around? If not, I'm going over to *Hosteen* Silver's place. I'm interviewing some more people for the handyman job this afternoon."

"Go. You may have to repair the front or back door, too, if he broke in," Daniel said, explaining. "There might also be some bullet holes."

"I'll head over there right now, take a look around and see what's what."

As Gene left in *Hosteen* Silver's old truck, Daniel led Holly inside. Though she'd shown herself to be a very resourceful partner, the toll these past few days had taken was etched on her face. There was a haunted look in her eyes, and as she moved he could see how tired she was.

He wished that he could have offered her that perfect, predictable life she seemed to want. Yet even the thought of living in a rigidly structured world gave him the willies.

They'd faced danger together, and had come out standing. As far as he was concerned, that was as perfect as things got.

"Holly, he won't win," he said, taking his hand in hers.

She squeezed it gently. "It's good to know you're on my side."

"Always."

Something tightened inside him. She could make him feel like one helluva man with that soft voice and those doe eyes. His brain crashed to a stop. He wanted her again.

"Let me wash up and then we'll head to the plant," she said, nodding toward the back rooms.

Forcing himself to stay where he was, he watched her walk away. The sway of her hips played on his memory and made his body ache. As she stepped out of view, he suddenly realized one thing. His world would never be the same without her.

HOLLY WASHED UP then took a bandanna from the top of a chair and fastened her auburn hair into a ponytail tied at the base of her neck.

It was time to go hunting for answers again. If Martin was the man behind the attacks on her, she needed to know why. It made no sense that a man she had a good working relationship with would suddenly want her dead. He'd even been the one to insist Daniel protect her. They had to be missing something.

Seeing a pair of boots by the closet, her thoughts drifted to Daniel. Even if heartbreak lay ahead for her, she would never regret the time she'd spent with him. He'd stood by her every step of the way. She'd never thought herself capable of trusting blindly, yet when she looked at Daniel, she knew with certainty that he would never betray her.

Love had made a place for itself inside her, and that feeling had redefined her and what she wanted in life. As far back as she could remember, she'd known what her ideal mate would be like, but that image was the opposite of everything Daniel was. So maybe perfection was overrated. Maybe the world created by Norman Rockwell was best left on canvas or on the cover of a magazine. After all, it lacked…reality.

"Are you about ready?" Daniel called out. "I tried calling Martin, but I can't get an answer, not even voice mail. Something's going on and I'd like to go take a look for myself."

She hurried down the hall and met him at the door leading into the front room.

He smiled as she joined him. "My bandanna looks good on you."

"You don't mind that I borrowed it?"

"You can wear anything of mine that fits you," he answered.

"I'll keep that in mind," she said and smiled.

They were in the truck and heading to the reservation's natural gas plant seconds later. All traces of playfulness were gone from Daniel's face. All she could see there now was tension and grim purpose.

"I've missed something. What's happened?" she asked.

"While you were in the shower, I spoke to Jerry Powell, the chief of security. He says that the police are there questioning Martin."

"Tribal police?" she asked.

He nodded. "Something about misappropriation of funds."

She expelled her breath in a soft hiss.

"You don't look surprised," he observed.

"I've often wondered about all his spending," she said. "Martin always seemed to have too much—a brand-new truck, a watch that cost a small fortune, the latest electronic gadgets."

"I thought his wife came from a wealthy family—the Markhams?"

"She does, and that's why I didn't dwell too much on it. One time he caught me looking at his watch and told me that it had been a gift from his wife. Though he was toying with his pen like crazy, and I wasn't convinced, I gave him the benefit of the doubt." She paused. "Yet even if he's guilty of embezzlement, that doesn't mean he's responsible for what's been happening to me."

"True, but I still want to talk to him," Daniel said.

"Do you think the tribal police will allow it?" she asked.

"Maybe, depending on who the lead investigator is."

They arrived a short while later and went directly to Martin's office. Martin was sitting at his desk, a uniformed officer at his side. A tribal police detective was speaking to Martin's attorney in the middle of the room.

"You've got nothing but a few accounting errors. Face it, Detective, that's just sloppy bookkeeping, not a crime," the attorney said.

"It's enough for a warrant, Mr. Eltsosie," the detective shot back, and nodded to another officer who'd just entered the room.

Martin, who'd nodded to Daniel and Holly when they entered, came over, followed closely by one of the uniformed officers. Holly noticed right away that Martin hadn't been cuffed.

"Don't look so concerned," Martin told Holly. "This will blow over. They've got nothing except a lot of hot air."

"We need to speak with Mr. Roanhorse," Daniel said, looking from Martin to the detective.

"As long as I'm standing here," the officer replied.

Martin rolled his eyes, then touched Holly on the arm for a second. "I heard what happened to you up there on the mountain. Are you two okay?"

"Yes, thank you for asking," she said.

"Here's what I want to know," Daniel said. "How could anyone hack into the tribal computer system, access your account, then download a specific file? We've got firewalls on the firewalls."

"After I spoke to your brother I decided to try and backtrack. Access logs show that my password was hacked, but the actual computer pathway used to download the file with your collection schedule belonged to my assistant. The problem is that

I spoke to Joe, and at the time the file was accessed, he was greeting guests at a reception we had here for some government officials. I was there, as well, so we can back up each other's alibi."

"So someone used Joe's computer without his knowledge, or cloned his IP address and made it look that way," Daniel said.

"Yeah, but that's not as hard as you might think. Joe's old school. He hates computers, so he doesn't generally bother with things like encryption. He also doesn't have a BlackBerry or any way to access his account here, except via his laptop, which he leaves on most of the time, by the way."

"Which, of course, begs the question, was the laptop spoofed, accessed remotely or did someone get into his office?" Holly asked.

"When we're both gone, we lock the office," Martin said. "Whoever did this hacked in from another location."

Holly glanced at the empty desk. "Where's Joe now?"

"The police wanted to search the place, so I told him he could take off for a while."

"Where is he likely to go?" Daniel asked.

Martin shrugged. "I honestly don't know, but he loves those glazed doughnuts at Tribal Perks. He'll go through a half dozen whenever he's on break."

"What's his cell phone number?" Holly asked.

Martin shook his head. "Won't help. That's it over there," he said, pointing to the device functioning as a paperweight at the moment. "When he takes a break, he takes a break."

The tribal police detective cleared his throat. "Sorry. I have to interrupt you three right now." He stepped up and cuffed Martin. "Mr. Roanhorse, you have the right to remain silent…."

"Don't worry," Eltsosie said. "I'll have you back out before dinner. They've got nothing on you."

Daniel and Holly left Martin's office shortly thereafter. As soon as they were out of earshot, she spoke.

"This may not have been Joe's fault, or have anything to do with him," Holly said as they walked back down the hall. "Johnny Wauneka is a more likely candidate. He has the skills to hack into almost anything. We need to find out if those two know each other, or have come into contact recently."

"You're thinking that Yazzie might have been tricked into compromising the password?" Daniel asked.

"Joe's a good, hardworking man and loyal to the tribe," she said. "Electronics just aren't his thing. He has a hard time understanding software."

"The way this went down still points to him," Daniel said. "Let's see if we can figure out where he is."

Daniel checked with security and was able to verify that Joe had left the parking area heading south about twenty minutes earlier. After getting Joe's home address, he glanced over at Holly. "His home's north of here, and so's Tribal Perks. Since he's not going to either, and he left his cell phone behind, we have no way of contacting him now."

"Then we'll talk to him when he comes back here. He will sooner or later. In the meantime, what do you say we go pay Johnny Wauneka a visit?"

"Okay, that's a good idea," Daniel said after a beat. "You want to take lead with him?"

"Yeah. Let me give it a try. Instead of coming on strong and accusing him of hacking and turning me into a target, I'm going to ask for his help. His reaction might tell us more than we'd get from a confrontation."

"All right. I'll keep an eye on him while you handle things. Let's see where this takes us."

Chapter Twenty-One

A long silence stretched out between them as Daniel settled behind the wheel and drove out of the gate, waving to the security guards.

"Why isn't anything about this mess simple? We should have more leads by now. We've had at least four separate run-ins with the guy after me," she said as they headed for the main highway.

"Conducting an investigation is like peeling an onion. There are many layers to get through."

"But does every layer have to reek?"

"No, but all too often, it does," he said, not taking his eyes off the road.

They arrived at Johnny's home sometime later. This time Daniel parked in front of the house itself rather than by the adjacent apartments. Today the place looked a little less like an abandoned home. That was mostly due to the tumbleweed snowman in the bare dirt front yard, and the simple pine wreath on the door.

"Christmas... I used to love decorating everything in my home. Bright colors can make anything sparkle," she said as they stepped up onto the concrete porch.

"Including my place?" Johnny said, opening the door and greeting them.

"Were you standing there, listening?" she asked, then saw him smile and shrug.

"I was staring out the window and saw you pull up," he answered. "So what brings you here?"

"Respect for your skill with computers," Holly said. "I'm hoping that you can help me with a problem."

"That depends. What do you need?"

"Someone hacked into a tribal computer. I need to know how that was done, by whom, if you can trace it and anything else you can tell me."

"Why should I help you?"

"I might be able to get you a job working with the tribe's IT people, making sure this kind of thing doesn't happen. You could come up with preventative measures, strategies, safeguards and firewalls. It's what you do best—and you'd be helping the tribe."

"And the natural gas plant."

"Yes. Up to now, I've told you that the tribal industries have nothing to hide, but it's clear to me you don't really believe that. If you have legitimate access to what's going on you could see that for yourself."

"Yes, but if I find that something important has been withheld from the people, my primary loyalty is to them."

"Fair enough—provided you don't pass along proprietary technology or private personnel records," Holly said.

"I can live with that. So tell me more about what's happened."

Holly gave him the short version of what she'd been going through, and how the hacker had tracked her.

"And you came to *me* for help?" he said, narrowing his eyes. "What makes you so sure I'm not responsible?"

"For one, you don't physically fit the description of the man after me," Holly said.

"How do you know I don't work for him?"

"I trust my instincts," she said quietly. "You work to protect, not to harm."

"Harming the few is sometimes necessary to protect the majority," he argued, watching her intently.

"You saved a rat, one of the least respected creatures, and you've spent all this time trying to convince me I shouldn't trust you. The opposite would have been true if you'd been out to do me harm."

He nodded, then moved over and took a seat at his computer keyboard. "Okay, I'll help you. Where would you like me to start? The facility's administration network?"

Holly nodded. "Someone hacked into a file that only two people have access to—Martin Roanhorse and his assistant, Joe Yazzie. We need to know who it was."

"All right. I'll start with Martin and Joe, since that's where the problem originates."

"Wait. Before you start, make sure you don't try to access Roanhorse's computer or files," Daniel said. "The police have him in custody and all his records are under scrutiny."

Johnny suddenly spun his chair around. "The *police* are involved? Are you trying to set me up?"

"If I were, I wouldn't have told you," Daniel said.

"What we'd like you to do is focus on Joe Yazzie's laptop computer and see if it was hacked," Holly said. "Can you do that for us?"

"Is there any chance the police will be monitoring him, as well?" Johnny asked.

"It's highly unlikely, at least not at first. Joe's not the subject of the investigation," Daniel said.

"We also know he isn't the person we're trying to find. Joe was greeting dignitaries at the time the file was accessed and downloaded, and the office was locked," Holly said.

"Then that means it was done remotely via the internet. So what you really need to know is *where* the hacker was at the time, how the file was downloaded and into which computer."

"Yeah, anything that will lead us to whomever stole that information," Holly said, giving Wauneka the name of the file, the exact time it was accessed and the password used. "I'm not sure if this will matter to you, but the password has probably been changed by now. They're supposed to do that weekly."

Johnny faced the computer, then glanced back at them. "That makes no difference to me. I'm not trying to read the file itself, I just need to access the computer user logs, which are in their local network mainframe. Could you move to the other side of the room please? You're jamming my personal space."

Daniel looked at Holly, eyebrows raised, then shrugged and moved back. Holly did the same.

After what seemed like a small eternity, Johnny glanced over his shoulder. "I've got something. The password you gave me was used to access and download the file you're interested in via a commercial business Wi-Fi. Are you sure you don't want a copy of the file?"

"I already know what's in there. I need to find the hacker," Holly said. "You said they gained access to Joe's computer via a commercial business Wi-Fi. Which one, and where?"

"Give me a minute," Johnny said. He typed several strokes, then changed screens a few times. "It looks like it happened at a coffee shop called the Tribal Perks."

Holly and Daniel exchanged glances.

"I'm guessing that Roanhorse and Yazzie visit that place?" Not waiting for an answer, he continued, "The hacker probably latched onto the current password while one or the other was sipping coffee and using an unprotected laptop. Old-school hackers use a keyboard logger program which keeps a record of the laptop keystrokes, and those give them the new password every time it changes. He could have uploaded the logger onto Yazzie's laptop if it wasn't secure enough."

"Thanks," Holly said. "I'll talk to a friend of mine at the plant, Jane Begay, and recommend that she put you under contract. She's always looking for good people."

"You could also consider coming to work for me," Daniel said. "I can use someone with your skills."

"I'm listening," he said.

"Let me get this case squared away, then we'll talk," Daniel said.

"I'll wait to hear from you," Johnny said, letting them out.

As they left Johnny's home, Holly glanced at Daniel. "We already know that Joe isn't very knowledgeable about computers. He may not have any idea that he's been hacked, or maybe he's involved. Either way, I think we should focus on him. For starters, we need to know how often he goes to Tribal Perks. With his careless use of the Wi-Fi connection, that makes him constantly vulnerable to a hacker."

"We may be able to cut corners and save time by studying the coffee shop's security video," Daniel said.

"I've been there on occasion, but I never realized they had security cameras there," she said.

"One of my brothers has just started his own business and talked them into updating their security after they got held up a month ago."

"So we'll talk to your brother first. Where does he live?"

He smiled. "Above the coffee shop. He's a close friend of the owner."

THEY ARRIVED at Tribal Perks a short time later. Instead of going to the front of the coffee shop, Daniel parked in the back beside a delivery truck.

"Should we call your brother and let him know that we're here?" she asked him.

"Paul already knows. That's why I parked where I did. He has this entire area staked out, and he knows Gene's pickup."

"Tell me more about Paul," Holly said.

"His full name is Paul Grayhorse, and up to a few months ago he was a U.S. Deputy Marshal. He's as tough as they come, but he's made some enemies while on the job. Paul's last assignment was in Washington, D.C., guarding a federal judge facing death threats. Long story short, Paul got shot saving the judge's life, so he took his disability and retired."

"Having an injury that ends your career is a lot for anyone to handle. How's he taking it?"

"It's been tough. Paul wasn't the only one wounded defending the judge. His partner was killed. Paul still blames himself for the other deputy's death, I think, but it's hard to say. None of my brothers are comfortable taking trips down memory lane."

"Just because you're men, doesn't mean you can't talk about your feelings."

"Yes, it does."

She glared at him.

"Just a heads-up before we go in. Paul doesn't like questions."

"Take the lead, then," she said. "I'll stay quiet."

He stopped at the bottom step leading up to the apartment and gave her an incredulous look.

"Okay, let's just say I'll be as quiet as I can."

Before they reached the top of the stairs a tall, broad shouldered Navajo man opened the door. He had penetrating black eyes that seemed to look right through her. Holly wasn't sure if he was smiling or snarling.

"Come in," he said, then waved them inside.

Holly studied him as she entered the room. Paul was wearing a gray wool round-necked sweater and a fetish hung from the leather cord around his neck. From what she could tell without getting a lot closer and being rude, Paul's spiritual brother was some kind of cat, perhaps the lynx. She tried to remember more about it, but all she could recall was that the animal was associated with secrets.

The two men bumped fists, then embraced briefly. "I've heard you're in a world of trouble right now," Paul said. "Is this the lady you've been keeping safe?"

Holly watched him for a moment. Paul moved with confidence, though she could tell he was favoring his right shoulder. Noting that he hadn't used a name, she smiled but didn't introduce herself.

Paul gazed at her for a moment longer, then gave her a nod. "It's all right to use Anglo names here. I go by Paul."

"Holly," she answered.

"We need your help," Daniel said, filling him in on the recent events that had led them there.

"I'll play back the feed on the café interior right now and see if we can zero in on your target."

"I appreciate this," Holly said.

"No problem. Daniel would do the same for me if I needed help. Otherwise, I'd have to pound his face into the dirt."

Daniel smiled. "You and what army?"

Holly took the seat Paul offered her and waited.

"I'm going back a month on this feed. I've already had the computer identify Joe's tribal ID photo and start to look for a match using facial recognition software."

As they waited, Holly looked around. Paul's tiny apartment was void of anything that might reveal something personal about him. Though she couldn't tell for sure, she had a feeling that was no accident. Like it was at Daniel's place, there was an absence of photos. She knew that some Traditionalists didn't like their photos taken, so that explained why they had none of *Hosteen* Silver, yet these were Modernist Navajo men. She was surprised that neither Daniel nor Paul had any photos of their other brothers, particularly since they were all so close, judging from what she'd seen so far.

Maybe, unlike her, they'd never felt the need for such mementos. She thought of the photos she'd lost in the fire. They'd held everything from pictures of the first table she'd set up to sell her rock creatures, to the last birthday she'd celebrated with her mom. She swallowed hard, knowing that there was no turning back the clock.

"Are you okay?" Daniel said, coming over to where she was sitting and offering her some coffee.

"I'm fine," she replied automatically, taking the offered mug. "I was just thinking of the photos I lost in the fire. Once I can go back and search, maybe I'll find some that are still salvageable."

"If you do, bring them to me," Paul said. "I'll do my best to restore them and upload the images into your computer so you can have instant access."

"I'd really appreciate it—that is, providing I find anything. Those photos meant a lot to me, so I'd be happy to pay for your work."

"Nah, I'd rather collect from my brother. He doesn't realize it yet, but he'll owe me big-time before we're done here."

Daniel burst out laughing.

Moments later, a tone sounded on the computer. Paul pointed to the split screen. "Here are the first six matches. From what I see here, Yazzie comes in at ten-thirty, then again at four—like clockwork. He sits in the booth by the south window each time—or the closest to it—has doughnuts, some coffee and works on that laptop. If he doesn't keep the firewall updated, grabbing his password wouldn't have been hard at all for an average hacker."

Holly stood behind Paul, looking at the image sections he'd delineated and placed side by side on the large monitor.

"Does anyone sitting around Yazzie look familiar to you?" Daniel asked her as his brother slowly advanced the images.

"That guy wearing the cap and sunglasses has been showing up on the most recent frames, but I can't make out his face. It's always shaded by the cap," Holly said.

Paul continued to advance the images. "The guy's kept a schedule that matches Yazzie's, but he always seems to keep his face down and his back to the camera."

"Either he's camera shy or someone determined to keep a low profile," Daniel said.

"I just noticed something, the first time he showed up was the day after I was attacked. Do either of you think that's a coincidence?" Holly asked, pointing at the screen.

"Let's see if we can spot him before then," Paul said.

They searched the two previous weeks, but they couldn't find anyone who seemed to fit.

"I wish there were better shots of that guy," she said, shaking her head.

"Maybe you can get a better look in person," Paul said. "If he stays on schedule Joe should be coming in about a half hour from now. Maybe his shadow will, too. Stick around, set up downstairs and see what happens."

"Good plan. I think he might be trying to get Joe's latest password," Daniel said. "Maybe Holly can ID him. The downside is that if he's our stalker, he's also bound to recognize Holly and me."

"Don't go in together just in case he comes early and sit separately. Holly can get a baseball cap and tuck her hair into it," Paul said, then looking at her, added, "Maybe you should also wear Daniel's leather jacket, too. It'll bulk you up a little."

"That should do it, particularly since he has no way of knowing we'll be here and won't be looking for trouble," Holly said.

"I'll sit across the room with my back to the camera. If he's avoiding getting caught on video, I should be safe enough," Daniel said. "I have a pair of yellow shooting glasses I can wear, as well, to alter my appearance."

"Reasonable. You two can stay in touch via phone. You have Bluetooths?" Paul asked.

She reached into her purse, and brought one out.

Daniel nodded, reaching into his pocket. "Looks like we're all set," he said, giving Holly his jacket as Paul handed her a Hartley Scorpions baseball cap.

"I'll be up here, keeping watch," Paul said. "If you need help, either of you, just touch your right earlobe and I'll come down."

"Your shoulder's still not healed," Daniel said, noting the way Paul favored it even while sitting. "I can handle this, but thanks for the offer."

"Anytime—I mean that."

"I know," Daniel said, bumping fists with his brother again. "I'll check in with you later, bro."

Chapter Twenty-Two

Once they reached the pickup, Daniel put on his yellow sunglasses, then backed out of the parking spot, waiting while Holly put on her disguise.

She leaned forward and stuck her auburn hair inside the cap, then pulled it low on her face. "Is Paul's fetish a lynx?" Seeing him nod, she continued, "I can't remember what the lynx stands for. Isn't it something to do with secrets?"

He nodded. "Lynx medicine allows a person to see what others don't, so he becomes one who can discern even the most highly guarded secrets."

"That fits with what you told me about him," she said.

After a brief silence, Daniel spoke, his mind back on the case. "I've been thinking of the guy with the cap," he said slowly. "He didn't seem to be Navajo, which tends to rule out all our best suspects."

"I know, and we already know it can't be Ross Williams," she said as he pulled to a stop.

"I won't be far," he said as she climbed out of the truck.

Holly walked in first. The coffee shop smelled of peppermint and pumpkin spice, two of her favorite flavors. With a laptop in hand, she bought herself a tall mug of coffee at the counter, then went to a corner table. No one looked in her direction once she was seated. Most people there were focused on their laptops, phones or on their companions.

Yazzie walked in less than five minutes later and sat in his usual booth. Daniel followed a minute afterward. He got himself a large black coffee, then went to a table, holding a newspaper.

"Anything interesting?" he asked, calling her on his phone via Bluetooth.

"Nothing yet," she said, looking up at the surveillance camera mounted near the ceiling to her right.

They waited, and within ten minutes, an Anglo man wearing a baseball cap walked in carrying a laptop. He stopped at the counter for a coffee, then sat one booth away from Yazzie, his back to the camera. He immediately opened his laptop and began to type, his head down.

"That could be the guy on the video. He's in profile, but I think I recognize him. I'm just not sure from where," she said.

"That's Arthur Larrabee," Daniel said a beat later. "We haven't considered him, but his body type fits our suspect, and when he crossed the room he had a trace of a limp—maybe the result of a rock slide?"

"Give me a few more minutes, then I'll leave through the side door," she said.

"Excellent idea, but I need to get out of here right now. If he spots me he'll know we're on to him. I'll be in Gene's truck, waiting," Daniel said.

Holly saw Daniel leave, then followed a minute or two later. As she reached the parking lot, Holly spoke into the Bluetooth. "There's a black Jeep parked here now that looks familiar. What caught my eye is the college parking sticker. I think this is the same Jeep I saw parked off the road when I was on my way to the plant—the same day I was attacked. Now that I think about it, Larrabee could have been the man I saw, except for the fact that the guy I saw out there had a beard."

"Larrabee had one before. He said it made his terrorist role-playing more credible. Then the day of the exercise, I noticed that he'd shaved it off. Interesting coincidence," Daniel said. "Point out the Jeep you were talking about, but don't wander over to it, keep walking to the pickup. I'm parked in the rear, near the stairs."

"It's the one to the right of the door. I remember seeing the red F college parking sticker that day. I assumed that the man was either an archeologist or a geologist looking for samples. The beard helped me complete the stereotype, I guess."

By the time Holly reached the pickup, Daniel was already talking to Gene on the phone.

"What did you get on the plate?" Holly asked Daniel after he hung up.

"It's registered to Arthur Larrabee all right," he answered. Daniel stared ahead for several seconds, gathering his thoughts, then glanced back at her. "How much do you remember about him?"

"He headed the opposing team during the training exercise. He's also running for city council in Hartley. What I can't do is say for sure that Larrabee is the person who came after me or tried to shoot us," she said. "I also have no idea why he would attack me. The Jeep certainly fits the one I saw, but that's hardly evidence of anything. The only thing we really have is that he appears to be the same man who sits close to Joe when he comes in, and that the shadowing began *after* I was attacked. If we could find proof that he's the hacker, we might be able to tie him to the rest of it."

"Yeah, but if he made us back there, he's going to start cleaning up. Larrabee's smart, so he'll make sure that there's no evidence left to tie him to the crime."

"I still don't know why I've become his target, but if he's really the one, we can't let him get away. We have to do something."

"We won't stop until you find justice."

She took a shaky breath. "If we're right about this, Larrabee will do his best to destroy both of us. We'll be part of what he's cleaning up."

"Think hard, Holly. Do you have *any* connection to Arthur

Larrabee—besides the fact that you saw him digging that morning?" Daniel said.

She paused before answering. "No, but I remember my friend Jane Begay told me that Larrabee's former girlfriend, Megan Olson, is missing and he was being questioned by the police. Martin was concerned because he didn't want any negative publicity, even by association."

"That's the first I've heard about that. Let me talk to Preston. He should be able to tell me what's going on with that case."

They went directly to the Hartley Police Station, and before long found their way to Preston's office. Preston looked up from his work station and gave them a quick half smile.

"You've been busy," Preston said. "I just heard from Paul. So what do you have for me?"

They both took a seat, then updated the detective.

"Larrabee's still a person of interest in the Olson missing person's case. Their breakup was really ugly, apparently, and she'd threatened to have him charged with abuse," Preston said, then focused his laser sharp gaze on her. "Are you *sure* he's the one you saw digging?"

She hesitated and Preston picked up on that instantly.

"You can't make a positive ID, can you?"

"No, and I didn't actually see him digging, either," she said, then explained. "Can you give me a good sharp photo of Larrabee and maybe add a beard to it? A well-trimmed beard, an inch long, tops."

"Let me pull up a photo we have on file," Preston said. He opened a facial recognition program, copied Larrabee's image onto the screen, and using the mouse, added a beard. Moments later, Preston turned the screen so she could see it.

Holly looked at the altered photo. "That's him. No doubt," she said. "He's the guy I saw by the Jeep."

"So why has Arthur been shadowing Joe Yazzie lately when he goes into Tribal Perks?" Preston asked.

"The only reason I can think of is that he needs to keep up

with the new passwords so he can access Joe's files and check on Holly's whereabouts," Daniel said.

"He could have hacked the password, which allowed him to learn our route, then find us in the woods," Holly added.

Preston stared at his desktop as if trying to make up his mind about something. After a moment, he stood, closed his office door, then returned to his desk.

"Off the record, okay?" He saw Daniel and Holly nod, then continued, "We've been after Larrabee for a while, but he's as slippery as a greased pig." Preston repositioned his computer screen, hit a few keys, then turned the screen back toward her. It was a Google Earth aerial view of the general area around the tribe's natural gas plant. He then pointed to the road she'd mentioned taking that fateful morning. "Can you identify the area where you saw him?"

"Right there," she said, pointing. "It's where the road turns back to the north. To the left of that is a dry arroyo and low ridge. Beyond, the ground slopes away to the west."

"This is on the Navajo Nation, so it's out of my turf," Preston said. "I'll contact the tribal police and send them an image with these coordinates. They're shorthanded, so I'm not sure when they'll get someone out there to check. It may take half a day."

"Larrabee's no one's fool. If he thinks we're on to him, he's not going to wait for the noose to tighten. He's going to move that body," Daniel said.

"I'll put some pressure on the request," Preston said with a nod, "but in the meantime, remember that Larrabee was a police officer at one time. He's armed and dangerous—not your usual suspect. Watch your backs."

By the time they were inside the truck, Holly's hands were shaking. She clutched them tightly but Daniel noticed and placed his hand over hers. "Are you okay?"

"No. I'm terrified that this man will slip away from us and I'll have to spend the rest of my life looking over my shoulder," she said, her voice rising. "I know what that's like, Daniel. I grew up with that kind of fear and I can't live my life that way again."

"It won't happen. If the police find Megan Olson's body at that location, things are going to come together fast."

"But what if he's already moved the body? Or worse, what if he left town after spotting us at the coffee shop? The police are going to need my testimony to link him to the crime even if they find the body, so he'll see me as a loose end he can't afford to ignore. Unless we catch him now, I'll never be able to have a normal life again."

Daniel said nothing for several long moments. "You've got a lot of courage, Holly, but are you really ready to do what's necessary to pressure him into making a mistake? It'll entail some serious risks, and the ability to act off the cuff. We can't stick to any particular plan, only a strategy."

She nodded. "I'm ready."

"Then let's do it. One way or the other, Art Larrabee's going down."

Chapter Twenty-Three

They arrived at a residential area filled with mostly older homes and southwest landscaped yards shortly after sundown. Though daylight was fading fast, it was still possible to see clearly.

"It's quiet here, like it was around my neighborhood—till I moved in," Holly said with a sad smile.

Though she was fighting to hold herself together, he could sense her fear. It drove him crazy to see her look like that. He couldn't breathe, he couldn't think. The need to protect her pounded through him like a fire in his blood.

He remembered the scared kid he'd been once, always over-compensating by trying to act tough. Experience had taught him that showing any weakness was like leaving a trail of blood in the woods. It turned you into instant prey.

Only someone who'd known terror firsthand could really understand what she was going through. Unrelenting fear ate you up from the inside out and that's what he saw in Holly's eyes and in her shaky smile. He could see how tightly she clung to her purse, protecting the one link she still had to her past. She was strong, but she'd been stripped of nearly everything that mattered to her and pushed to the breaking point.

Larrabee was a lethal adversary who knew how to zero in on his opponent's vulnerabilities and who would strike with precision and without mercy. Daniel wasn't afraid for himself, but the thought of anything happening to Holly made him go cold inside. She was his weakness, and if Larrabee ever discovered that, he'd use it to bring both of them down.

"That's Larrabee's home, the one at the end of the cul-de-sac," Daniel said after a moment.

"It backs up against the *bosque* trail. Nice place," she said wistfully. "When I first started looking for a home, I tried to buy one in this neighborhood, but I couldn't afford it. I had this dream…" Her voice trailed off.

"Don't stop there," he said, parking at the curb several doors down from Larrabee's house. From their location, he could keep three sides of the house under constant surveillance. "Tell me about your dream."

"I wanted to own a place with some land so I could get a horse." She gave him a sheepish smile. "It would have had to have been an extremely gentle animal, because the last time I went riding I was seven and the pony was being led by its owner."

He smiled. "If you move into the cabin you could buy a horse. There's plenty of space for one. Or you could borrow one from Gene and see how it works out for you."

Holly shook her head. "I can't plan that far ahead." She stopped, blinked and gave him a startled look. "Did I really say that?" She let her breath out in a sigh. "I used to plan *everything.* I could tell you exactly where I wanted to be ten years down the line." She smiled slowly. "You know, I've wasted a lot of time on dreams."

"There's nothing wrong with having dreams."

"Maybe there is, if you spend so much time creating them that you forget that life isn't really something any of us can control." She paused. "I've learned a lot—about myself, about what's important—since this all started."

His gaze held hers. "Maybe we both have. I'm not a man of fancy words, Holly, but…I'll stick with you no matter what happens," he said at last. He'd meant to tell her that he loved her, but the words had gotten all tangled up in his throat. A man who was a man didn't talk mush—his actions showed what was in his heart. Surely that was enough, wasn't it?

She leaned over and kissed him. It was a tender kiss, filled with sweetness and longings. Then she whispered something in his ear. Stunned, he sat frozen. Had she just told him that she loved him? Before he could say a word, she opened the door and started walking down the sidewalk toward Larrabee's house.

He hurried after her and pulled her aside, behind a tree. "Are you crazy? What the hell do you think you're doing?" Even as the words came out of his mouth, he realized that this wasn't at all what he'd wanted to say…or do.

"There are no signs that he's been here lately. Several newspapers are on the front lawn, and no lights are on inside. Let's take a closer look. The house next to his is up for sale, so if any neighbor comes out and asks, we can say we're shopping for a home."

"Slow down," he said, grabbing her hand. Though he'd stopped in front of the house for sale, his focus was on Larrabee's property.

"Oops, my mistake. He *has* been here," she said, gesturing with her chin.

He followed her gaze. The Jeep she'd seen with the college parking sticker was parked in the alley at the back of the property, just beside a gate in the chain-link fence.

"He was smart enough to hide it back there, his only option since he doesn't have a garage," he said.

"So he must know we're on to him. He might be inside—"

"Hello, young people," an elderly woman said, coming out of the house they'd just walked past. She was holding a surly, squash-nosed bundle of brown hair that barked and growled at them. "Don't mind Mr. T. He's cranky to strangers at first, but he warms up eventually. Just don't try and pet him."

"Wouldn't dream of it," Daniel muttered.

"He's a beautiful little dog. And look how protective he is!" Holly said, ignoring the crinkled snout and razor-sharp teeth.

The woman smiled. "He's a great companion. Are you interested in the Sanchezes' home? The bank foreclosed on it last month and the asking price is very reasonable."

"We've been looking for a place," Holly said.

Daniel watched her. Holly could brighten anyone's day with that smile. He quickly brought his thoughts back to business. "We'd like to get a feel for the neighborhood, so it's good to talk to you," he said. "What about the people who live there?" He pointed to Larrabee's place. "Are they friendly, like you?"

"Mr. Larrabee has always been a very private person and we've never talked that much, not until recently. He's running for city council now, and wants my vote, I guess. I'm sure he'd like to meet you—if you're a registered voter in this district."

"Maybe we should go and introduce ourselves," Holly said, squeezing Daniel's hand.

"He's not there right now. He came by earlier, parked his Jeep out back, then left in his truck. He's hardly ever at home, so as far as neighbors go, he shouldn't be a problem for anyone."

She looked at Daniel, then at Holly. "It would be nice to have another young couple, and maybe children running around here again. With the Sanchezes gone, it's been too quiet."

The thought nearly squeezed the air from Daniel's lungs, but Holly seemed to take it in stride. "I like what I've seen of the neighborhood so far, but I think I'm going to walk around a bit, maybe check out the back of the property and the area beyond that," she said. "I like hiking in the *bosque*."

"What's back there is mostly a horse trail," she said. "By the way, my name's Susie Kane. I've lived here practically all my life, so if you have any questions, come by tomorrow. Right now I've got to go. It's bingo night at church and Mr. T and I are already late."

The woman walked over to her white sedan, placed the dog on the seat beside her, then drove off moments later.

"Good work," Daniel told Holly. "Now let's go around to the back and see what we can find. Just don't touch anything. If we compromise any evidence, it'll work against us."

"Don't worry, I won't touch a thing."

They walked down Larrabee's concrete driveway, then crossed into the backyard. "Hey, let's take a look in that window," she said. "The curtains aren't drawn."

Without waiting for him, she hurried over. "There's a fatigue jacket hung from a hook, and on the door mat I can see a pair of boots with some reddish mud on them."

He came up and glanced inside. "You're too close. Back up a bit," he said, not wanting to have her accidentally come into contact with anything, especially the window glass.

"Do you think that'll be enough for a judge to issue a search warrant?"

"I doubt it. When it comes down to it, all we have is mud and a Jeep. It still falls short of probable cause."

She curled both hands into fists and clutched her purse against her. "This guy gets all the breaks!"

"No, not all. We *are* getting someplace, and it's picking up speed."

She moved over to look through the smaller kitchen window, angling to get a better view. "There's a box in there, Daniel, and a photo on top of it. Is that me at one of the press conferences?"

He came up beside her. "It looks like a printout, and it's too grainy to tell for sure who that is at this distance."

"But it could be me. Isn't that enough for a court order?"

"A photo of someone we *think* might be you?" He shook his head. "Probably not, especially because he was officially at the gas plant for training ops. That could be part of a publicity kit he picked up there."

"Daniel, we can't just ignore it. Maybe we can find a way inside," she said.

"No."

"Let me at least try the doorknob," she said.

"*Stop.* Don't do anything."

Daniel stepped back and looked around. There was a tan

truck parked at the side of the curb about three doors down. The driver, a man with a bill low over his eyes, was sitting there, watching them.

Daniel moved closer to Holly, his instinct for danger going on high alert. He was inches from the door when he caught the scent of rotten eggs—or worse. As he glanced inside the kitchen, he saw that the oven door was open.

"There's something else on top of that box, beside the photo. I think it's a phone," Holly said.

As he heard a ring he felt a burst of adrenaline shoot through him. "Run!" He grabbed Holly's hand, yanked her away from the door and raced away from the house.

They'd gone less than thirty feet when an explosion ripped through the air, throwing them face forward onto the ground in a wave of heat and flame.

"Stay down!" he said, pulling her against him.

Bits and pieces of wood, glass and roofing showered all around them, some of the debris on fire.

"What…" she managed, then ducked her head into his chest as big chunks of wood and insulation rained down on them.

"He was watching the house—and us. I caught the scent of gas, and when the phone rang I knew. A spark was all he needed."

They crawled away from the heat and flames, then finally Daniel turned to look. After waiting a moment longer, he stood and gave her a hand up.

"He blew up his own house!" she said in an awed whisper, looking at the smoking hole blasted out of the kitchen. It looked like an artillery strike.

"He also destroyed whatever evidence was inside. This guy knows precisely what he's doing." Daniel grabbed his phone, called Preston and briefed him, raising his voice to be heard over the wail of approaching sirens.

"Yeah, we were set up," Daniel said. "The fire marshal will undoubtedly find evidence of arson inside. To me, this looks like an act of desperation, so I'm sure he knows we're closing in."

"Did you see the make and color of his vehicle?" Preston asked him.

"He was driving a tan truck, extended cab. His neighbor, Susie Kane, might be able to give you more details."

"I'll run his name through DMV. Meanwhile, bring Holly here and we'll take your statements."

"No, taking Holly to the station's *not* a good idea," Daniel said. "That's what Larrabee's expecting me to do. He has a rifle and could pick us off outside the entrance or along the way. In fact, he may already be in position. I think we should stay on the move and remain unpredictable while you put out a BOLO on this guy. He can't pin Holly or me down if we're constantly in motion. I'll stay in touch."

"I'll check credit card usage, ATMs and also see if his cell phone is on so we can get a warrant and track him. Watch yourselves in the meantime."

Daniel closed up the phone and placed it back in his pocket.

"I heard what you said, but how long can we keep moving?" she asked as they hurried back to the pickup. A fire truck was coming up the street from the opposite direction, and several residents were on their lawns, looking at the smoldering house and the oncoming emergency vehicle.

"All night, if necessary. There's a BOLO out now, so every law enforcement agency in the county will be on the lookout for him."

"Sounds like it's going to be a long night," she said as they got under way.

"Yeah, but look at it this way. By Christmas this might all be over."

"Tomorrow's Christmas Eve. That's not a lot of time," she said.

"Either way, you and I can still have a special Christmas."

She smiled. "We'll have to decorate…something."

He smiled slowly. "I'll keep that in mind."

Her eyes grew wide, and she looked away, her cheeks flushed.

He smiled again, then after a moment grew serious. "After I make sure we're really in the clear, I'm going to arrange to meet Preston away from the station. I have an idea."

Chapter Twenty-Four

Twenty minutes later, they were on their way to meet Preston. As they pulled into a gas station off west Main Street, the detective was already there, waiting.

"I took a roundabout way here, doubling back, just to make sure we were clear," Daniel said, handing Preston the keys to Gene's pickup. "Here you go. Treat it gently or he'll have your hide."

"You mean he'll *try*," Preston said, his eyes filled with mischief.

"One more thing. How about trading cell phones with me, too?"

"Yeah, good idea. Anyone can find you on a GPS if they have your number and the right hardware," Preston said. "And you can't afford to stay out of contact."

"Guys, I hate to point this out, but by switching pickups and phones, all we've done is give Larrabee a new target—Preston," Holly said.

Preston flashed her a mirthless, lethal smile. "I'm so hoping you're right."

"My brother will have lots of backup and be ready to party," Daniel said.

Preston looked at Holly, his gaze gentling slightly. "There's more to this than catching the bad guy. It's about standing up and being counted when one of my brothers has his neck on the line. It's about honoring *Hosteen* Silver's legacy."

As Daniel and Holly got into Preston's Explorer, Holly glanced at him. "How do *you* define *Hosteen* Silver's legacy?"

He took a deep breath. "The most important lesson he taught us is that blood ties don't make a real family. Genes and DNA are just scientific markers that belong in a lab, but ties of the spirit last forever. Our family was forged by the strength of one man. We honor him by being the men he knew we'd become." He took her hand, but said nothing more.

She'd wanted a picture-perfect hearth and home, but these past few days she'd learned that what she'd truly yearned for couldn't be found in a building. She had no home, and her future was in question, yet beside Daniel, she'd found peace and love. Perhaps she'd never hear the words "I love you" from him, but his heart had whispered it to her in a language that didn't need sound.

"For the first time in my life I'm truly beginning to understand what walking in beauty is all about," she said.

He looked at her for a fleeting moment, then kissed her hand. "Let's finish what we set out to do—make sure the dirtbag after you spends his holiday behind bars. Afterward, you and I will have our own well-deserved Christmas celebration."

She smiled. Not exactly *I love you,* but it would do.

THEY TOOK TURNS DRIVING, avoiding the major streets and roads whenever possible. They stopped to pick up coffee a few times, but only caught a few hours of sleep here and there. By morning, the constant pressure had taken its toll.

"I'm so beat, I feel like a zombie," Holly said, rubbing her eyes and trying to stretch in her seat, knowing it was her turn to drive.

"Fortunately for me, you don't look like one," he said, pulling over to the curb.

She laughed. "Did I hear you talking to Gene a little while ago?"

"Yeah, he and Paul have been watching our backs, making

sure we didn't pick up any unexpected company. Paul didn't have to do this. The guy's not ready for field work, but he insisted on giving Gene a hand with surveillance."

"They both love you."

Daniel opened his door. "Your turn to take the wheel."

It was cold, and she slid over past the center console to take his place as he hurried around the front of the Explorer.

"What is it with you guys?" she asked as he hopped in and fastened his shoulder belt. "You'd face a gunman without so much as a blink, but any talk about emotions and feelings and you run for cover?"

"Not so. You ever watch guys watching a football game?" he said. "You've never seen so much love or hate going on in your life. And talk about showing their emotions...."

"You know what I mean. You're being evasive."

"Am I?"

She put the Explorer in gear, checked her rearview mirror, then pulled back out onto the street. "Never mind."

Later, as the clock on the dash turned to six-thirty, Holly stopped at the drive-up window of a fast-food joint. They picked up breakfast burritos for both of them—and more coffee.

Moments later they were eating, parked in front of a school. As sunrise began to appear from over their right shoulders, the cell phone Preston had given Daniel rang.

Daniel placed it on speaker as Preston identified himself. "We just got a call from the tribal police," he said. "The officer assigned to examine the possible dig site Holly pinpointed for us wants her to meet him there. After the recent storm it's hard to find disturbed ground. He needs her help in narrowing down the location."

"That came directly through police channels?" Daniel asked.

"Yeah, and I double-checked before calling you. It's legit. Officer Benally said he's parked just off the left side of the road. When you get close you should be able to spot his unit."

"Copy that." Daniel turned to Holly. "You ready for this?"

"You bet," she said with a nod.

"Let me make sure we've got backup standing by. A few added precautions can't hurt," he said, then dialed Gene.

Forty minutes later, they turned up the same dirt road she'd taken that fateful morning. The sun was still low in the sky as Holly's gaze took in the layer of frost that covered the high spots in the dirt road. It was Christmas Eve, a good day for Megan Olson's family to finally find closure, and with that, peace.

She leaned forward and pointed to her left. "There's a white tribal SUV about a hundred yards ahead. Officer Benally's in the right spot—the old tire tracks left by the Jeep are still visible."

Daniel reached for the cell phone, then as he turned off the road to follow the tire tracks, spoke to Gene. "We're here. If there's any news, I'll call you back."

As Daniel ended the call, Holly tensed. "I don't see Officer Benally anywhere." She shaded her eyes as she looked to the east, directly into the sun.

Daniel parked and reached for his jacket. "The vegetation is pretty thick right around here, so he may have decided to expand his search over that rise while waiting for us."

Holly zipped up her coat as she followed Daniel along the fresh and days-old tire tracks toward the white tribal unit. "The day I saw Larrabee out here, his Jeep was right over there," she said, pointing. "See the wide, faded tracks? He had some kind of big tool bag. At least that's what I thought it was...."

"Good memory," Larrabee said, stepping out from behind the tribal SUV. He had a semiautomatic pistol pointed at Daniel. "That's why I knew I had to get rid of you, but you know the whole story now, don't you?"

Daniel slid his right hand down toward his waist.

"Don't tempt me, Hawk. I'm not playing laser tag and this

is no training exercise. Keep your hands up where I can see them."

Holly felt her heart hammering against her side. Taking a breath and trying to sound calm, she asked the question foremost in her mind. "What did you do to Officer Benally?"

"He's taking a nap over there," Larrabee said, cocking his head toward a cluster of thick brush on the far side of the SUV. "We can keep talking, but if that duct tape turns out to be too tight over his mouth, he may suffocate while we watch."

"What do you want, Larrabee?" Daniel growled.

"Use two fingers of your left hand and take out your pistol, then set it down gently on the hood of your vehicle. Cooperate, or I'll cap you, your new girlfriend and Officer Benally, in that order."

"Why should we do what you say?" Holly said, surprised by how steady her voice sounded, particularly because she was almost sure she was going to be sick. "You're going to kill us all anyway."

"Maybe yes, maybe no," Larrabee said, moving the pistol back and forth between them. "I can't stay in this area anymore, no matter what happens, so cooperate and I might let you see Christmas."

"You killed Megan Olson and buried her out here—but where exactly?" Holly said, wanting to stall and keep him talking.

"Let me guess, once I answer, you're going to insist you've recorded it on your cell phone," Larrabee said, then sneered. "This isn't some stupid TV cop show, it's the real deal, so don't try playing games with a professional. Last chance, Hawk. Put the gun down—*now*," he ordered, walking slowly toward Daniel as he cocked the hammer of the pistol.

Daniel did as Larrabee asked, never taking his eyes off the man.

"Now take two more steps back, Hawk, or I'll kill the woman right now. I was on the pistol team back in the day, so

I can put two rounds into her face before she takes her next breath."

Larrabee picked up Daniel's pistol, then eased the cocked hammer of his own weapon and tucked it into his belt.

Moving with slow deliberation, he aimed the barrel of Daniel's gun directly at Holly. "Kneel on the ground. You, too, Hawk. I'll make this quick and clean."

"No," Holly managed, standing up tall and trying unsuccessfully not to shake. "If I'm going to die, there's no way I'll do it on my knees. I'll stand."

"Caw!" The incredibly loud cry of a bird came from somewhere behind them. Larrabee instinctively turned his head to look, and Daniel made his move.

Seeing Daniel coming, Larrabee pulled the trigger. Nothing happened, not even a click. Larrabee looked down at the weapon just as Daniel tackled him.

Both men fell back onto the frozen ground and Daniel's pistol landed somewhere behind them. "Get my gun," Daniel shouted to Holly.

Larrabee grabbed Daniel by the throat, but Daniel kneed the big man in the groin and Larrabee's grip relaxed. As Daniel punched Larrabee, Holly ran over and picked up the gun. Why hadn't it fired? Maybe it wasn't loaded. She looked down for the safety, and found a little lever with a red dot showing. Should she move it?

As she turned around, Daniel was still on top of Larrabee, who was kicking up off the ground, trying to throw Daniel off. Larrabee's pistol was knocked free during the struggle, landing several feet from the men, but with Daniel continuing to throw jabs, it posed no threat to either man.

Holly moved closer. If the two separated even for a second, she'd have a shot—that was providing the gun decided to work this time.

"I'll take that if you want, Holly," a familiar voice said.

Holly jumped, saw it was Gene coming up from behind and gladly handed him the pistol.

Daniel threw one more punch, and Larrabee stopped struggling, out cold.

Daniel picked up Larrabee's lost pistol then stood. "A bird call, bro? Was that the best you could do?" Daniel said, looking over at Gene, a ghost of a smile on his face. "Were you that afraid to come out of hiding?"

Gene laughed. "I figured you'd want to take him down by yourself."

"Yeah, I've never been good at sharing."

Gene grinned. "I noticed you used that old safety trick *Hosteen* Silver taught us. Saved your life, didn't it?" Gene pulled back the slide of Daniel's pistol, feeding a round into the chamber and cocking the weapon.

"'*Never* have a round in the chamber of a semiauto until you're ready to shoot. Safety first.' I can still hear his words," Daniel said.

Holly looked back at the tribal vehicle. "We need to find Officer Benally."

While Gene watched their still-unconscious prisoner, Holly and Daniel went to look for the tribal officer. They found him struggling to sit up a few feet from his unit. Holly pulled off the tape that covered his mouth as Daniel used his pocketknife to cut the clothesline binding his wrists and legs.

"What the hell happened? I heard a noise, got clocked from behind and the next thing I know, I'm trussed up like a calf."

Daniel updated him. "Your attacker is out for the count right now, but we could use your cuffs," he added, gesturing to where Gene was guarding Larrabee.

Benally reached for his belt. "I'll handle it," he said, walking over to Larrabee, who was starting to regain consciousness. Giving him a look of utter contempt, the tribal officer rolled him onto his face and fastened the cuffs. "This is the man you saw out here?" he asked, looking up at Holly.

She nodded. "That's him. He was over there by those rocks at one point." She pointed to the location.

"Are you sure about that? Think back carefully," Daniel said.

Holly closed her eyes for a moment, trying to recall the details of that day. "I remember these rocks," she said, picturing everything in her mind's eye.

After Benally placed Larrabee in the back of his tribal unit, the four of them spread out. "The ground here hasn't been disturbed at all," Daniel said, studying the area.

"It's *got* to be here. I'm sure I'm right." As Holly glanced back, she saw Larrabee watching and smiling, despite his bruised face.

"Maybe he moved the body already," Gene said. "If he did, it could be anywhere—miles away, or burned beyond recognition."

"No. If he'd already moved the body, he wouldn't have seen me as a threat, and continued to come after me," Holly said. "It's here—somewhere."

After twenty minutes, Benally looked over at them. "It's not here. It's impossible to completely hide a grave. Even taking into account the past storm, the ground would still show some telltale signs. If nothing else, we'd see where the earth was mounded or sunken in."

"He ambushed you at this location and took you hostage for a reason, Officer Benally," she insisted.

Panic rose inside her as she suddenly considered the possibility that Larrabee would once again slip out of their grasp and elude justice. Forcing herself to focus, she turned in a circle, taking in everything around them.

"There's one more possibility," she said, looking at Benally. "You followed the directions to this general area, but why did you park where you did?"

"I saw tracks that indicated a vehicle had been parked there."

"I think that was precisely what Larrabee was counting on," she said.

Daniel smiled. "I see where you're headed with this. He wouldn't have risked burying a body exactly where you saw him, but he wouldn't have wanted to lug it around, either. It was already morning and there was more traffic coming on the roads."

"Exactly," Holly said. "Officer Benally, would you move your SUV back onto the road for us?"

"You're thinking that he moved his own vehicle back and buried her right where he'd parked his car?" Benally asked.

"Yes, and it was a good plan, too," Holly said. "If anyone else came in afterward to look around, they'd probably park in the same place he had since it's the only clear spot this far from the road."

Larrabee stared at them, but said nothing as Benally moved the tribal unit about twenty feet back. Daniel, Holly and Gene went to the spot Benally had exposed and studied the ground.

"The sand here has been disturbed, then smoothed over in a hurry," she said.

"You're right, and look over here," Daniel said, pointing. "You can see a few recent, smooth, flattened marks about the width of a shovel."

"Leaves and twigs have been sprinkled along the top and spread out evenly to hide the smoothing of the ground, but none of them are even partially buried," Gene said. "Nothing's growing here, either, not even a blade of grass."

"Anyone got a shovel handy?" Daniel asked.

"I've got one in my vehicle," Gene answered.

"So do I. Let's start scooping away the dirt, but work slowly and carefully," Benally said. "If we find any evidence of a body, we stop and turn it over to the crime scene people."

"What can I do?" Holly asked, not really wanting to see what was left of the dead woman.

"Go to high ground and see if you can spot Larrabee's tan pickup," Daniel suggested.

Holly nodded. "Good idea. He didn't walk here."

SWEEPING ASIDE SAND and working through the many layers, Benally soon uncovered a hint of clothing and a human hand. By then, Holly had returned and was watching the men dig.

"Everyone step back. There's a body here," the Navajo officer said.

"It's a female," Daniel said, looking down into the shallow grave. "She was wearing a turquoise bracelet." He gestured to a string of turquoise beads clearly visible on the withered wrist.

As much as she wanted to, Holly couldn't look away. She whispered a prayer, knowing in her heart who'd really paid the ultimate price in this tragedy. Her own losses had been so inconsequential when she compared them to what had happened to this poor woman. "Her family—it turns out they were right about Larrabee," she finally managed, wiping angry tears from her eyes. "They need to know."

"They'll be notified," Benally said, bringing his cell phone up to his ear.

"So this was the reason he came after me," Holly said, turning to look at the man in the car. "My life was the price of his secret."

"Larrabee's going down, and where he's headed he'll never pose a danger to you or anyone else again," Daniel said, placing his arm over her shoulders and pulling her close to his side.

Epilogue

Daniel and Holly arrived at the old cabin well after sunset. As they pulled up, Holly saw the unmistakable twinkle of Christmas lights in the window. There were three vehicles parked around the cabin, one she recognized right away as the old pickup Gene had been driving.

"Who else besides Gene is here?" she asked, seeing people inside.

"My other brothers—the ones who live in the area, that is. Kyle and Rick weren't able to make it this year," Daniel said. "It doesn't always work out for all of us, but we try to get together during the holidays and on special occasions. I know you like Christmas celebrations, so I thought you'd enjoy spending it with us."

A family Christmas and she was being included. A special warmth filled her as they climbed out of the truck and she heard laughter coming from inside the cabin. "I have a feeling this is going to be my best Christmas ever."

As they walked into the house, the odor of burnt…something…wafted across the room.

"The turkey wasn't quite thawed out when I put it in the oven, so it's kind of overcooked on the outside," Gene said.

"What he's really saying is that it was hard as a rock when he blasted it in the oven," Paul said. "But don't worry. We're taking up the slack with skillet-cooked scrambled eggs and pancakes."

"But they'll be Christmas pancakes," Gene said. "I used

food coloring and swirled the batter with green and red before Preston could get to it."

She burst out laughing. "Let me help."

"Nah, we've got this. You two have been through enough," Preston said, poking his head out of the kitchen. "Paul, I can use your help. Gene, you, too."

Holly started to follow, but Daniel grabbed her hand gently and pulled her over in front of the roaring fireplace. "I've been wanting to say something to you. Now that we're alone...well, at least in this room...."

She waited, looking at the small, decorated pine tree in the corner, balanced in a gravel-and-water filled galvanized bucket. They'd done their best to decorate it with a single strand of lights, brightly colored glass balls, homemade, carved wooden ornaments and aluminum foil stars.

"About your home—you can rebuild," he began, searching for the words.

"I know. Sometimes, I guess, old dreams need to be shattered before you can rebuild and begin anew," she said. "But what about you? Will you still be around?"

"My work may take me away at times, but your home, *our* home," Daniel whispered, "will be the same if you'll have me."

Suddenly someone in the kitchen yelled "hot" and dropped a metal pan. That was followed by loud laughter. She laughed, too. Somehow, it all felt right here. A family bound by the power of one extraordinary man—*Hosteen* Silver.

"Look, it's snowing," Daniel said, bringing her attention back to him.

"Come on, bro. Man up! Tell her you love her already," Gene called out.

Daniel shot a hard glare in the direction of the kitchen, but it had suddenly grown very silent in there. "Can we go outside for a moment?" Daniel asked.

She nodded, reaching for his hand.

Outside, it was as quiet as could be. As a gentle dusting of snow continued to fall, he reached into his jacket pocket and pulled out a card. "I'm not a man of words, so I got you this. You can open it and hear what's in my heart anytime you want."

She took the card. It was the kind that featured a personal, recorded greeting.

"I bought it for you a few days ago, and I've kept it in my jacket pocket, waiting for just the right time. Hopefully it still works after that fight with Larrabee."

She opened it breathlessly. Daniel's deep, rough voice came out clearly at first. "Sweetheart, I—" Then there was a pause, as if the recording had hiccupped and the words "love you with all my heart," followed in a rushed, high-pitched cartoon voice.

Holly stared at the card, and heard the raucous laughter coming from the cabin.

"Why don't you give it another try?" Holly asked, gazing up into his eyes.

"Kiss her, you dummy!" came Paul's voice.

Ignoring his brothers, he held her gaze. "I love you, Holly," he whispered. "Be mine."

"I am," she answered, as his lips gently sealed hers.

* * * * *

SUSPENSE

Heartstopping stories of intrigue and mystery—
where true love always triumphs.

Harlequin®

INTRIGUE

COMING NEXT MONTH
AVAILABLE DECEMBER 6, 2011

#1317 BABY BATTALION
Daddy Corps
Cassie Miles

#1318 DADDY BOMBSHELL
Situation: Christmas
Lisa Childs

#1319 DADE
The Lawmen of Silver Creek Ranch
Delores Fossen

#1320 TOP GUN GUARDIAN
Brothers in Arms
Carol Ericson

#1321 NANNY 911
The Precinct: SWAT
Julie Miller

#1322 BEAR CLAW BODYGUARD
Bear Claw Creek Crime Lab
Jessica Andersen

You can find more information on upcoming Harlequin® titles,
free excerpts and more at www.HarlequinInsideRomance.com.

HICNM1111